LEGACY OF THE LIGHT

Legacy of the Light

Library of Congress Control Number: 2026904744

ISBN: 979-8-234-00081-1 (Paperback)

Printed in the United States of America

First Edition: 2026

Also by Cymarshall Law

52 Laws of Freedom - A Weekly guide to Raw Self
Expression and Mental Health

I Still Love H.E.R.

LEGACY OF THE LIGHT

— A Novel —

Cymarshall Law

To my children—

Tyshar, Azari, Nyari, and Orion.

You are my greatest accomplishments,

my brightest stars,

my living legacy of light.

Remember always:

The world doesn't come at you.

It comes from you.

Table of Contents

Bump in the Night..1

Solid as a Rock... 8

You Don't Have to Believe in Fire................................. 14

Walk It Like It's Already Ours....................................24

Two Storms, Same Direction..32

Becoming..41

Move the Room, Shift the Culture..................................49

Pressure Point Poetry... 59

Cracking the Air Open... 64

The Kick Heard Around the Universe................................ 69

The Chune of Your Soul.. 77

What You Do After Fear Speaks..................................... 83

Try Me in Stereo..88

The Beat That Built It.. 94

Rhythm and Ruin...102

Pages of the Same Verse...111

Wings and Beacons... 117

One Beat, Three Directions..123

The Ones Who Sharpen the Blade.................................... 128

Where the Silence Trains You...................................... 137

Back Into Light... 145

The Whisper That Breaks the Circle................................ 149

Where the Concrete Hums... 157

The Arrow That Hesitated.. 162

Where the Future Waited...168

Catching Up to Prophecy... 174

The Symphony of the Unfinished.................................... 179

The Sound of Betrayal...184

The Betrayer and the Beat.. 190

Surrender or Symphony...194

The Rhythm That Ended Fire...................................... 200

The Last Whisper Before Tomorrow........................... 210

Rhythm Is a Weapon Too...215

The Last Verse Before The Storm................................ 225

ABOUT THE AUTHOR... 228

FOREWORD

This story has lived with me longer than most memories.

Before it had a name, before it had characters, before it had planets and prophecies, it existed as a feeling—something ancient, something familiar, something calling me from the edges of imagination.

I began writing **Legacy of the Light** in pieces back in 2006, though I didn't know it at the time. It showed up in my music first—in the story songs I created like *The Alchemist*, *SuperGirl*, *Bump in the Night*, and *100 Years*. Every time I wrote a verse that felt like a movie, every time I closed my eyes and saw a world behind the beat, I was really writing this book.

Growing up, English class was my sanctuary. It was the one place where imagination wasn't just allowed—it was required. That love for storytelling carried me across oceans, into studios, onto stages around the world. Hip hop became my passport, my compass, my way of translating the visions in my mind into something people could feel.

But this story—this one—comes from deeper roots.

It comes from Jamaica, where my family began.

It comes from England, where I was shaped.

It comes from America, where I became myself.

As a kid from the UK with West Indian blood growing up in the U.S., I rarely saw stories that reflected my experience. Yet our culture—our sound, our slang, our rhythm—has always been woven into the DNA of hip hop and American life. Still, our stories were missing. Our voices were missing. Our heroes were missing.

This book is my answer to that silence.

It is also a tribute to my father—the man who introduced me to sci-fi, comic books, and the mysteries of the unknown. The last movie we ever watched together was *Elysium*. He is the reason music lives in me. He is the reason we came to America in 1990. He is the reason I learned to dream beyond borders.

In many ways, **Legacy of the Light** is the story of my family disguised as cosmic mythology.

It is the journey of diaspora turned into prophecy.

It is the battle between darkness and light that every generation must face.

It is everything I love—hip hop, martial arts, sci-fi, spirituality, ancestry—woven into one universe.

This book is my heart.

This book is my story.

This book is my legacy of light.

— **Cymarshall Law**

1

Bump in the Night

"A people without knowledge of their past is like a tree without roots." — Marcus Garvey

The heavens smoldered.

Twin moons cast an eerie light over Everlion, a planet cracking beneath the weight of endless war. Plasma bolts tore through the sky like vengeful comets. Shattered citadels burned in silence, their ruins whispering the names of the fallen. A Damlya warship — sleek, monstrous, leaking shadow energy — spiraled through a crystal ridge, its hull groaning with hunger.

Across the battlefield, the Warriors of Light descended like prophecy incarnate. Beaming swords in hand, they moved with elegance and fury, their strikes humming with sacred rhythm. Light clashed with shadow. Hope with hunger. The war had no end — only echoes.

Beneath the chaos, time slowed.

In a hidden cave lit by glowing roots, Azariah leaned against the jagged wall. His armor was scorched. One horn cracked. His charcoal skin shimmered with blood — not red, but radiant, leaking energy that pulsed like a dying star. Each breath was a battle.

Before him stood Novi.

Golden-eyed. Robed in light. Fierce and gentle. She was everything the war had forgotten. She cupped his face, her touch soft against the storm.

"We don't belong here," she whispered.

Azariah's voice was low, resolute. "No. But neither does this war."

"If they find us…" Her voice trembled. "They'll kill you. Kill us both."

"Then let them try."

He pulled her into an embrace. Their foreheads touched. For a moment, the war faded. Only love remained.

"I'll burn this planet," Azariah said, "before I let them take what's mine."

The mountain rumbled above them.

She shed a golden tear. Vulnerable. True.

"They'll call it betrayal," she said. "But I feel… like we're the only ones not lying."

Azariah reached into his chestplate and withdrew a golden pendant, softly vibrating. He placed it in her hand.

"For him."

She stared at it. Another tear slipped down her cheek.

"You still believe in the prophecy?"

"I have to," he said. "He'll live. We will live —
through him."

A shockwave quaked the mountain. Dust sifted from
the ceiling. Outside, muffled shouts grew louder.

Novi drew her blade. It vibrated in her grip with a
sacred hum.

"He's still so quiet," she said. "Too quiet."

"He listens... like you. He already feels the weight."

They scrambled down through jagged terrain to a
small spacecraft, its core pulsing softly like a heartbeat.

Then came the growl.

Three Damlya Hunters burst from a rocky ridge,
armor glinting, weapons buzzing with energy. Azariah
snarled, lifted his arm, and conjured a dark matter shield
midair. It shattered on contact with a hurled spear.

"No more hiding."

He unslung a double-bladed staff. FOOSH — it
ignited in a flash of blue flame.

"Take him," he said. "Get to the ship. Now."

"Azariah, no—"

"There is no future for him... if we don't fight for it."

He leaned in. Kissed her forehead. His fingers grazed
Zorion's cheek — the baby's skin flickered with faint
golden glow.

Novi trembled, but nodded.

"Then go," Azariah said. "Protect our son. I'll hold them off."

She clutched the pendant. Her body turned gold as she phased out in a flash of blinding light.

A split second later, three Damlya Elite stormed the cave, weapons raised.

Azariah turned. His fangs bared. His blade ignited.

"You want prophecy?" he growled. "Come bleed for it."

—

The ridge trembled beneath Novi's feet.

Fire rained from the sky. The mountain cracked with fury. She sprinted across the war-torn plateau, cradling Zorion against her chest. The baby stirred — silent, sensing the storm behind them. Explosions erupted in the distance — Azariah's final stand.

The ship door hissed open.

Novi leapt inside, breath ragged, eyes burning with grief and resolve. Her fingers danced across the controls as she whispered the ancient tongue.

"Esh'tu lavaya... Earth."

By starlight, be free.

The engine roared. A blinding explosion lit the ridge behind them — Azariah's sacrifice etched into the sky. The craft tore through the atmosphere, breaching the stars. A meteor streak followed in its wake, as if the cosmos bore witness.

—

Earth shimmered below, cloaked in moonlight.

The Blue Mountains of Jamaica rose like sleeping giants. Fireflies stirred. Frogs chirped. The world slept.

Novi gazed out the window, Zorion nestled in her arms. His skin glowed faintly, the prophecy pulsing within him.

She knew the mission had only just begun.

—

Dawn broke in a clearing.

Birdsong began — soft, sacred. Novi stepped from the ship, now in human form. Barefoot. Regal. Wrapped in worn Caribbean cloth. She held Zorion close as he stirred. The air was thick with rhythm.

She listened.

The rustle of leaves. A distant drumbeat. A goat's bleat. A pot clanging. The wind humming through banana trees.

It wasn't noise.

It was pattern.

It was pulse.

"This world," she whispered, "is full of music. Even its silence has rhythm."

She looked toward the valley below. A small village stirred to life — smoke rising, voices waking, the day beginning.

On Everlion, music wasn't entertainment. It was memory. It was how they passed down the Laws — through vibration, through breath. Every note carried a truth. Every harmony, a history.

She knelt, placing Zorion gently on the soft earth.

"Your father fought in silence," she said. "But you... you will rise in sound. Because music is movement. And movement is will."

She touched his chest, feeling the quiet power within.

"You'll need that music to find your way. To remember who you are when the world tries to rewrite you."

A rooster crowed. A child laughed in the distance.

"Let the rhythm guide you, my son," she whispered. "Even when the light dims... sing."

She rose.

The wind lifted her wrap.

The prophecy had begun.

They disappeared into the jungle — and into Earth's story.

2

Solid as a Rock

"The child who is not embraced by the village will burn it down to feel its warmth." — African Proverb

Jamaica. Years later.

The sun rose over Montego Bay like a blessing.

Lush hills glistened beneath its light, mist lifting from the trees as if the island itself were exhaling. Waves crashed in the distance. Goats bleated. A pickup bassline hummed through the air, vibrating in the soil.

The rhythm of life stirred — not just sound, but soul.

Zorion grew in that rhythm.

—

At six, he watched fishermen cast nets into the sea, their movements fluid, ancestral. A nearby radio played Sizzla's "Solid As a Rock," the instrumental echoing across the water. Zorion held a shell like a microphone, mimicking their cadence, his voice rising with the tide.

At thirteen, he helped wire a sound system for a local dance. His fingers moved with instinct. But when he touched a cable, a flicker of blue light escaped his hand.

He froze.

Looked around.

No one noticed.

The rhythm continued.

—

At eighteen, he was DJ Natty Dread.

He commanded the street dance beneath swaying palms and colored lights. The crowd pulsed with energy, chanting his name between sound clash rounds.

"Gwan Natty Dread! Brapp Brapp Brapp! Yess Poppa Natty Dread!"

The music blared. Curry-scented air thickened. Spliffs passed. The basement bashment was shocking out.

Crystal entered the party, eyes scanning the dance. He paused, smiled, and whispered one word:

"Timeless."

He walked to the mic, catching a head nod from Natty Dread.

The rhythm was sacred.

The night was alive.

—

Then Rudy stormed in.

Two cronies flanked him, armshouse energy thick in the air. His voice cut through the music.

"You think say yuh better dan me?! Yuh can't DJ in my street dem? Now everyting will be nice if you just pay the price..."

He reached for a Crocodile Dundee-style blade — abnormally large, gleaming under the party lights.

Zorion stood firm.

"Tonight is for di people," he said. "Play unu set and gwaan easy."

Rudy snarled.

He shoved Zorion hard into a speaker stack.

Gasps rippled through the crowd.

"Yuh soft, Natty. Let me show dem who run dis."

He swung the machete — wild, reckless — aimed at Zorion's chest.

Zorion dodged, barely.

The blade sliced through a speaker cable, sparking violently.

"Yo! Rudy, chill!" Crystal shouted.

But Rudy lunged again — this time with intent.

The crowd began to panic.

—

Zorion's eyes flashed white-gold.

He lifted his palm, instinctively.

A pulse of silent energy blasted out — invisible, but powerful.

Rudy and his boys were thrown back.

Not just physically.

Spiritually.

Lights blew.

Amps sizzled.

The air warped.

The crowd froze.

Rudy hit the ground hard. His blade skidded across the pavement. His cronies scrambled, bouncing fast, eyes wide with terror.

A woman in the crowd whispered:

"Dat... dat was no obeah. That bwoy him nah normal..."

Whispers rippled.

Fear.

Awe.

Confusion.

—

Novi's house. Night.

Her fingers trembled as she packed.

Zorion paced the floor.

"I couldn't help it," he said. "I didn't want to…"

"What we are," she said softly, "will always find its way out."

She pulled open a floorboard and retrieved a gold pendant, glowing softly.

"They'll be coming," she said. "The Damlyas… they felt it."

She locked eyes with him.

"You faced your fear. Now we must face the fire."

—

Airport. Dawn.

Two silhouettes vanished into the departure gate.

The Caribbean hills bathed in orange light, watching them go.

This was 1970.

The rhythm shifted.

The prophecy moved forward.

3

You Don't Have to Believe in Fire

"When the roots are deep, there is no reason to fear the wind." — African Proverb

London, 1993.

A cool mist clung to the edges of the football pitch.

The match was in its dying moments — Eastside 1, Visitors 1 — and tension rippled through the crowd like static. Bleachers shook with chants and stomps. The air was thick with anticipation.

Ty stood on the left wing, hands on hips, sweat dripping. His eyes flicked to the sideline.

Sakira smiled at him, mouthing: *You got this.*

The midfielder passed.

Ty took the ball and danced — hips fluid, rhythm effortless.

One defender.

Then another.

The crowd surged.

Then — **BAM.**

A brutal shoulder check sent him sprawling into the mud. The ball rolled loose. Groans echoed.

Above him stood Gavin.

Tall. Smirking. Tattoos peeking from under his sleeve.

"Oi… Sakira tastes like Cheerios, fam."

Ty blinked.

That phrase pierced something ancient.

Something buried.

Then — **BOOM.**

His body glowed.

Ambient gold.

Subtle at first, but enough for gasps to rise from the crowd.

In the bleachers, Novi dropped her thermos.

"Rahtid!"

Nyah turned to Zorion.

"Do something, before he levels the whole postcode."

Zorion's voice was calm. Urgent.

"No. Let him finish this."

On the field, Ty stood.

Steady.

Powerful.

Even Gavin stepped back.

Ty dashed.

The turf exploded underfoot. Cleats left craters as he launched forward, catching the ball in stride.

He cut.

Juked.

Spun.

But it was more than skill.

It was a dance of light.

A rhythm older than the game.

Silence.

Then — **FWOOOOOM.**

The ball rocketed like a bullet, warping the air, shattering the net in the upper corner.

Goal.

The crossbar wobbled.

The keeper stumbled.

The crowd froze.

Then — eruption.

Friends rushed the field.

But Ty just stood there, glowing, staring at his hands.

That wasn't just instinct, he thought. *That was something else...*

From the bleachers, Zorion was already leaving.

"We move now," he whispered.

—

Three days later.

The sun slinked behind high-rises on a South London block alive with flavor.

Afro-Caribbean shops pumped dancehall rhythms into the street. A grill smoked jerk chicken on the curb. A cypher echoed nearby — kids trading bars with patois peppered in.

Ty shadowboxed alone in golden hour light, headphones on.

His rhythm — part street, part stardust.

Molded by hip-hop.

Sharpened by something older.

—

His room was a sanctuary.

Big L. Bruce Lee. Lauryn. Fugees.

A boombox that wheezed soul.

On the wall, a scroll with glowing glyphs — partially hidden behind posters, but watching.

Ty rewound an old VHS: *Ancient Flow: Vol I.*

He copied a movement.

Wobbled.

Fell.

"Man… this prophecy thing's fi wasteman," he muttered. "Nobody glows in real life, Pops. That game? I probably just blacked out. Nothing mystical agwan."

—

Rooftop. Twilight.

Cityscape below. Pink-orange sky above.

Ty leaned on the ledge, catching his breath.

Zorion joined him.

Older now.

Eyes heavy with secrets.

A man who'd lived war and waited for peace.

He held a weathered envelope.

"You remember how I used to tell you the prophecy might be about me?"

Ty half-laughed.

"Used to? You still say it like you're the chosen one."

"I did believe that," Zorion said. "Trained like it. Bled like it. But watching you on that field... when you glowed... when time itself bent around you..."

He sighed.

Looked out.

"That's when I knew for sure. The prophecy wasn't about me, Ty. It's always been you."

Ty turned.

Disbelief.

Dread.

"That was... adrenaline. Heat of the moment. Ain't no 'chosen' in my bars and beats, Dad."

"You've got rhythm, yes," Zorion said. "But what's pulsing underneath is older than rhythm. Everlion.

Warrior and Damlya. The blood of Azariah and Novi flows through you. Every technique I taught you — the forms, the breathing — that wasn't just training. It was an activation."

He handed Ty the envelope.

Thick.

Ty opened it.

Stunned.

"Yo. What is this?"

"Enough to get you across the ocean. New Jersey. There's someone — Jazz. She's from our side. She'll take you in."

Ty hesitated.

"Wait... you serious? You want me to just chip? Just go?"

"I want you to live, Ty. To grow into all of what you are — artist, fighter, beacon. Your dream's been America since you were ten. Music's your voice. But now your power is your amplifier. After the energy you left off the other day... the Damlyas are definitely on their way. Unless you go, we're all in danger."

Ty looked down at the bills.

Then out across the skyline.

"So... you just happened to come into this money?"

Zorion smirked.

"Let's just say the universe settles old debts when it's time."

Ty nodded.

Processing.

The moment heavy.

Sacred.

"Pack light," Zorion said. "But take everything I taught you. The world is listening — for your voice and your glow."

"You rob a bank, old man?"

Zorion chuckled.

Turned serious.

Smiled.

—

Days earlier.

A bank door kicked open.

Gritty UK Garage thumped through the air.

Zorion moved like he'd seen the blueprint.

Calm.

Methodical.

Bigs stumbled in behind, carrying a gym bag that said *Bad Bwoy Swim Team MVP*.

Flea burst in after — small, hyped, waving a pink pistol.

"Please tell me that's not the gun I think it is," Zorion muttered.

"Got it on clearance!" Flea beamed. "Half price, two for one. Comes in rose gold too."

"You robbing a bank or auditioning for Barbie's bodyguard?"

Customers dropped.

The teller hit the panic button.

Zorion moved like clockwork — over the counter, wires unplugged in seconds.

"Don't worry, love," he said. "We're professionals. Allegedly."

—

Alley. Minutes later.

They tumbled out, sprinting toward an old Vauxhall with two hubcaps and no shame.

Bigs, breathless, eating a sandwich:

"That went... surprisingly decent?"

"You brought bread. Flea brought Barbie's sidearm. We're a documentary waiting to happen."

—

Getaway car. Moving.

Flea swerved like he was playing Mario Kart.

Bigs counted money like it was Monopoly.

"Where to?"

"Anywhere with no CCTV and good curry, mate."

—

Back to the rooftop.

"No," Zorion said. "Let's just say... the universe finally paid me back."

Ty stared at him. Uncertain.

"You really believe it? That I'm chosen?"

Zorion placed a hand on his shoulder.

"You don't have to believe in fire... for it to burn."

Ty's grip on the envelope tightened.

A quiet decision formed.

4

Walk It Like It's Already Ours

"Every mickle mek a muckle." — Jamaican Proverb

The bassline rolled in like memory.

"She Keeps On Passin' Me By" played low — chopped horns and dusty drums filling the room like incense. Ty's bedroom was a teenage sanctuary: cluttered, sacred, alive.

Cassette tapes spilled across the dresser. Vinyl sleeves leaned against the wall. Posters of Nas, Guru, RZA, and Bruce Lee watched over him like ancestral spirits. A book titled *Flow: Ancient Motion Theory* lay cracked open beside a half-eaten beef patty.

Ty bopped his head in sync, toothbrush in mouth, shadowboxing half-dressed. His movements had grace — fluid like water, unpredictable like jazz.

He froze.

The polaroid on the mirror caught his eye.

Sakira.

Her smile. Her big earrings. Her eyes.

The beat dropped.

She walked through a hallway misted in soft gold light, mouthing his name. He stood in a cipher, methodically bodying a freestyled verse. She watched from the edge, lips curled in a smile.

Ty blinked back to reality.

Grinned sheepishly.

Fixed his collar like she was already watching.

He threw on his backpack, glanced at his kung fu gi hanging by the door, and nodded at his reflection.

"Today... let's walk it like it's already ours."

He hit stop on the tape deck, grabbed a spiral notebook labeled *Verse Science Vol. 3*, and stepped into the hallway.

—

The kitchen buzzed with rhythm.

Muffled patois floated from the phone. The smell of frying plantains drifted through the air. Novi hummed softly as she stirred the pan.

Ty tapped her shoulder.

"Morning, Super-Gran. How are you?"

He kissed her and his little sister Daizja on the cheek.

"I'm alright, baby," she smiled.

"Mumsy!" he called to Nyah.

Nyah held the phone to her ear, then paused.

"Whal on, whal on… TY, you know everyday I am fantastic and improving, my love."

She hung up, sensing something in his tone.

"Yes Mum, just checkin', init?"

He hesitated.

"So… I spoke to Dad last night. He said you lot came together and… said I should go America. To live."

Nyah held his hands.

Novi finished cooking and joined them at the table.

"Yes," Nyah said. "We all think it's time. We know you were meant for greater things. And we feel now is the right time to see what the world has to offer you."

Ty nodded slowly.

"If you all think it's the right thing for me to do… then I'll do it."

"We have a friend in New Jersey," Nyah said. "You can live with her until you get settled."

"OK Mum…"

Novi and Nyah smiled.

They embraced him.

"I'm off to the dojo now," Ty said. "I'll see you lot later, yea? Love."

Nyah waved goodbye, already returning to her conversation with Novi.

The kitchen buzzed with quiet warmth.

—

The dojo was alive.

Sunlight poured through long warehouse windows. Dust drifted like ancestral spirits. Incense coiled in the air — shea butter, sandalwood, ambition.

Ty and Sakira faced each other on the mat, both in worn black gis. Sweat beaded on their foreheads. Their stances low. Eyes locked.

They bowed.

And ignited.

Sakira leapt into a fighting stance — inside crescent, then wheel kick.

Ty ducked, spun into a sweeping leg strike.

She vaulted over it, landing clean in cat stance, smirking.

Ty charged — double strike to the ribs, elbow feint, spinning back kick.

Sakira bent into a butterfly twist, her braids slicing air like commas in motion. She landed clean, dropped low, caught Ty's ankle mid-step, flipped him over her shoulder.

He hit the mat with a thud.

Grinning.

"Practicing with Jet Li again?" he panted.

"Nah," she said, circling. "Bruce. Be water, my G."

The crowd quieted.

Students leaned forward.

—

Steam hissed from a bus's undercarriage.

Streetlamps flickered in the fog.

Yvonne stepped off, lifting her headwrap against the drizzle. Denzil followed with a battered suitcase.

Toots & The Maytals played faintly from a nearby cab radio.

"So... this is the Kingdom," Yvonne said.

"Feels more like the Kingdom of Damp," Denzil muttered.

A punk walked by with a boombox blasting ska. A chip van hissed behind them.

"You think they got ackee 'round here?"

"Hope so. Otherwise I crossed the Atlantic for mashed potatoes and misery."

She almost smiled.

—

Ty's stance deepened.

Something ancestral flickered in his breath.

He launched — aerial cartwheel, tornado roundhouse kick with snapping precision.

Sakira blocked, rolled, and in a flash delivered a full twisting corkscrew through the air.

Landed on one leg.

The crowd gasped.

"That all-natural?" Ty asked.

"Organic power," she grinned. "No additives."

They went again — palm strikes, inside traps, low sweep, kip-up, slide-through counter.

She flipped off the wall.

He dove beneath her, sweeping.

Like two dancers possessed by rhythm and memory.

—

Young Ty and Sakira sparred playfully in the grass.

Barefoot kicks.

Ice cream melting on the bench beside them.

"You know my folks came over in '70, right?" Sakira said. "Just tryna escape the madness back home."

"Same year mine landed," Ty replied. "Windrush kids raised on rice 'n peas and kung fu flicks."

—

Their bout continued — grappling, punching, a blend of modern kung fu and Jamaican footwork.

Their rhythm was intimate.

Primal.

The dojo seemed to disappear as their energy took over.

Ty meditated beside his father, Zorion, in full gi.

Zorion corrected his posture with a stick.

"Your body is the key," Zorion said. "But your mind... that's the sword."

Teen Ty punched a dummy until his knuckles bled.

—

Ty threw a tiger claw strike.

Sakira blocked.

Countered.

Ty evaded, moved in fluid motion, escaped swiftly.

His eyes glowed — just for a moment.

Sakira noticed, but said nothing.

"You're different now," she said, catching her breath. "Sharper."

"You too."

"College preps. Life stress. Training with Sensei G in Tottenham. You?"

—

A ten-year-old Ty trained under the stars.

Zorion stood before him in silence.

"The body is a tool, yes," he said. "But the spirit, the intention... that's the blade. You walk with it. You don't swing it wildly. You move light. You move with Law."

—

Sweat flew.

The sparring intensified.

Ty's breathing deepened.

He moved differently — his strikes smooth, spiritual.

The prophecy pulsed beneath the surface.

5

Two Storms, Same Direction

"A single arrow is easily broken, but not ten in a bundle."
— Tibetan Proverb

The dojo held its breath.

Sweat shimmered on the mat. The sparring slowed. Ty and Sakira stood in silence — breath sharp, eyes locked.

"I'm leaving," Ty said quietly. "Jersey. Mum says it's time. Dad's been cryptic, talking like the next chapter's already written. Says I need to finish what he started."

Sakira didn't blink.

She stepped back, rolled her shoulder. Her voice was calm, but loaded.

"I know."

Ty's brow furrowed.

"You know?"

"I got into Rutgers. Honors track. I leave in two weeks."

The air shifted.

Less surprise.

More suspicion.

"You didn't think to mention that?"

"I didn't owe you that," she said. "Besides, I needed to see if you were still moving like a student… or like someone who's ready."

"Ready for what?"

"For the real world. For the weight. London's been loud, yeah, but I'm not escaping it. I'm expanding. I've got mentors in Jersey. People who see what I'm building. I'm not following you, Ty. I'm building my own warpath."

Ty's jaw tightened.

He was recalibrating.

"So this isn't fate?"

"Fate's for people who wait around," she said. "This is alignment. Two storms, same direction. Doesn't mean we're the same."

—

Little Sakira danced on the carpet.

Denzil manned the decks at a house party.

Yvonne pulled her close and whispered in her ear:

"You are the dream your granny packed in a suitcase. But dreams don't float. They fight."

—

Back in the dojo, Ty nodded slowly.

"So we land in Jersey. Not as kids. As weapons."

"I'm not a weapon," Sakira said. "I'm the architect."

She threw one last spinning kick.

Ty caught it mid-air.

Their eyes locked.

No smiles.

No softness.

"Whatever's coming," she said, dead serious, "you ready?"

"I'm not just ready," Ty said. "I'm chosen."

They clasped hands.

Not in triumph.

In pact.

Two forces.

Two migrations.

One collision course.

—

Ty stepped out into the London chill.

Headphones on.

Steam rising off his skin.

"One Love" looped softly on his Walkman.

Tracksuit half-zipped.

His spiral notebook — *Verse Science Vol. 3* — tucked under his arm like scripture.

The streets of South London moved in rhythm around him.

Aunties argued over plantains and yellow yam prices.

A man sold incense and VHS kung fu bootlegs from a milk crate.

School kids cussed each other in thick, rapid-fire jokes.

Everybody got cracked on.

Miss B swept her stoop.

"That same tape again, Ty? Give it a rest, nuh."

Ty pulled off his headphones.

"Never gets old, Miss B. It's like Sunday dinner with lyrics, innit?"

He walked on.

—

He was in a queue at Heathrow.

Passport clenched.

Nerves bubbling.

Two rows ahead, Sakira laughed with her mum.

They locked eyes — brief, electric.

Funny how some people land in your life... before you even know they're staying.

—

Ty slipped into his last-ever form class.

A few heads turned.

Someone clapped once.

Jamal and Shaq made space.

"Look who it is," Jamal grinned. "Bruce Lee with the BARS."

"Man's hairline is levitating though," Shaq added. "Balding from all that inner chi."

Ty laughed, dropped his bag.

"You lot couldn't land a punch in Tekken if I paused the game for you."

"But you love us though," Jamal said.

Ty bumped fists with the boys.

The teacher wasn't even in yet.

It was that kind of class.

"So... what's this I hear about you cutting out?" Shaq asked.

"Jersey," Ty said. "Flying out this weekend."

The banter thinned.

Realisation dawned.

"Swear down?" Jamal asked quietly.

"Zorion sorted it. Got people out there. Said it's time to see what the world's saying."

"You going from chicken and chips to... what? Dunkin' Donuts and detention?"

"Back in Year 12 over there. American high school."

"Wait — mans gotta go back to school after we graduating here?!"

"Yes, man."

They all burst out laughing.

Shaq wiped a mock tear.

"Our boy's evolving still. Next time we see him, he'll be rapping with a Yankees cap and a sus New York accent."

"Nah… never that, ya eeediat," Ty said. "I'm taking ends with me."

—

The cafeteria was loud.

Packed.

Smelled like chips, spilled beans, and ambition.

Ty and the crew posted up in the corner by the radiator — Jamal, Shaq, Lola, and Anthony.

Lola eyed Ty's Walkman.

"So what, you gonna drop a mixtape first term and ghost us when you're famous?"

"You'll be my first diss track, Lola. Promise."

"You better namecheck ends at least," Anthony said. "From Brixton to Brick City, yeah?"

Shaq put on a mock American accent.

"Yo, I grew up rough in London, where the mandem will check you and the weather's disrespectful."

They all howled laughing.

A moment of joy they didn't know was precious.

"But for real," Jamal said, serious now. "We're proud of you, fam."

"I'll miss this," Ty said. "The cussing. The mandem. You lot kept me breathing when the air got thin."

He dabbed his eyes like he was joking.

He wasn't.

"Write us into the bars," Lola said softly. "Don't let America whitewash your soul."

"I'm going to raise the flag in every freestyle," Ty said. "Promise."

They fist bumped, one by one.

"Go fly, bruv," Anthony called out. "Just don't forget who tuned the wings."

—

Ty stepped out through the school gates one last time.

Kids poured past him in uniforms and ambition.

He lingered.

A flicker.

—

Ty stood on a stadium stage.

Twenty years old.

A sea of lighters before him.

Mic in hand.

Sakira beside him in white.

You don't chase dreams. You walk 'em on a leash.

—

Back in the present, he exhaled.

"Let's go walk this thing, yeah?"

6

Becoming

"It is better to have less thunder in the mouth and more lightning in the hand." — Apache Proverb

Rain dotted the windshield.

Zorion drove in silence, calm but unreadable. Mist curled across the London streets like memory. In the backseat, Ty sat with his duffel and Walkman, headphones half-on, beat low. Early De La. Maybe *Stakes Is High*, Spinna remix. Something that felt like goodbye.

"Feels weird," he murmured. "Like I'm not packing clothes. I'm packing versions of me."

Novi smiled gently from the backseat, where she sat next to Daizja who seemed like she'd seen this movie.

"That's because you are. The boy. The man. The warrior. And the question mark you haven't met yet."

Nyah rode shotgun, eyes red but chin up. Novi hummed an old Nyabinghi chant under her breath. The car rolled toward Heathrow.

—

At the curb, Ty adjusted his backpack.

The terminal loomed behind him, dawn light bleeding through glass.

They hugged in layers.

"Wherever you land," Nyah said, cupping his cheek, "make it home. And don't let the world tell you what you are — you teach it."

Novi held his face close.

"Walk like your ancestors paid the fare."

"They did," Ty said.

He looked back toward the departure gate.

Zorion stood behind the glass, hand raised.

Go walk your dream, son. Don't chase it. Walk it on a leash.

Ty nodded.

Then disappeared into the gate.

—

Security.

Passport in hand.

He hesitated.

Looked back.

His family was still watching.

He raised a fist.

They raised one back.

—

On the plane, Ty wore a Bartman T-shirt.

Calm.

Alert.

Cautious.

He found his window seat, buckled in, and closed his eyes.

Funny thing about leaping into the unknown, he thought. *You can't take your soil with you. But sometimes... your roots stretch anyway.*

Quick flashes:

Yvonne and Denzil arriving in London.

Sakira mid-spin in the dojo.

Zorion's hands demonstrating a crane stance.

Miss B sweeping stoops, mouthing Nas lyrics.

Lola whispering: *Don't let America whitewash your soul.*

—

Newark Airport. Customs line.

Ty stepped off the plane, collected his luggage.

An officer blocked his path.

"Come with me. You've been chosen for random selection."

"Random what?"

"We're just gonna need to check through your luggage."

"For what? Didn't you need to do that to get the bags on the plane already?"

The officer said nothing.

Just stared.

"Anything I need to be worried about in the bag?"

"Someone snapping a picture of you touching up mans draws."

The officer grimaced.

Checked the bag.

Found nothing.

Ty sucked his teeth.

"Purpose of visit?"

"To live. To rap. To fight. To figure out the rest."

"Student visa?"

"...Yeah. That too."

Stamp.

—

Outside, Newark air hit him — loud, greasy, alive.

Sirens howled.

Taxis cursed.

It smelled like ambition and concrete.

HONK-HONK.

A red Jeep rolled up.

Jazz leaned across the wheel.

"Yo! London Boy!"

Ty jogged up.

"You drive?"

"Only with purpose. Get in."

—

Boom-bap hummed through the speakers.

Black Moon.

Jazz ate fries without offering any.

"So you're the British Blade."

"That what they're calling me?"

"Nah. That's just what I saw when you stepped out that terminal. You've got that... glimmer."

"I'm just trying not to get arrested for my accent."

"You're not in London anymore. Over here, light's got to be sharp. World tries to steal it."

"Then I'll make it blinding."

He smiled.

First real one.

"You'll be staying in the spare room at mine. I'm out in the morning helping at the shelter, so you'll have to find your own way to school. I'll show you the way."

"No probs. I'd like to get to know my new ends anyway."

"Your ends?" Jazz chuckled. "Your first day at Newark High starts tomorrow. You'll find your way soon enough. Some of us have been waiting for you."

—

The Jeep glided through the steel heartbeat of New Jersey.

Graffiti sprawled across overpasses.

A kid spun on cardboard outside a bodega.

A mural of Chino XL watched over it all.

They said crossing oceans would test me, Ty thought. *Maybe I'm not just crossing… maybe I'm becoming.*

Redman's *Tonight's Da Night* instrumental rode shotgun.

The Jeep pulled up to a weathered apartment building — faded bricks, iron bars, stubborn resilience.

They stepped into a rickety elevator.

It groaned and climbed toward the seventh floor.

—

The apartment was modest.

Clean, if lived-in.

Cracked tiles.

Scent of Pine-Sol.

The quiet hum of city life just outside the window.

Jazz gestured.

"So… this is it. Not much, but it's home. Your folks helped mine back in the day. Debts and favors and… karma, I guess. So for now, it's your home, too."

"Thank you. Really. I don't take this for granted. Soon as I get things moving with the music, I'll be out of your way, I promise. I got some new material, new styles, cadences, flows I've been working on if you wanna hear anytime?"

"Nah. Don't even worry about that right now. Get settled. This one's yours."

She pointed to the spare room.

"Yo — your first day of school tomorrow. Get some sleep."

They bumped fists.

A moment of energy.

A quiet acknowledgment.

Ty stepped inside the room, threw his bag on the bed, and took a breath.

—

The next morning.

Ty stood outside Newark High.

Another new place.

Another beginning.

If he wanted the dream, it started here.

7

Move the Room, Shift the Culture

"The flame that burns twice as bright burns half as long."
— Chinese Proverb

The school bus rolled through Newark like a beat on loop.

Ty sat alone, middle row, hoodie half-zipped, eyes on the window. His accent and silence cloaked him like armor. Brick buildings blurred past — barbershops, corner bodegas, murals of Big L and Queen Latifah watching over the streets.

He exhaled.

Flashes of memory flickered behind his eyes: Zorion on the rooftop, handing him the envelope. Sakira's smirk, fading into light. A golden flicker in his palm on the football pitch.

Redman's drums thumped in his head. Pete Rock's *Half Man Half Amazing* instrumental played in his mind.

Then came the voice.

"Yo! Spit ya best verse then! You wanna battle?! I'm right here!"

Heads turned.

In the back row, a crowd huddled — Dante and Jamal among them, mid-cypher. The tension rose.

"Ladies first," Dante grinned. "Go head. Let the Queen cook."

The energy shifted.

At the center: Rico.

Tall. Cocky. Iced out in fake gold. A Newark kid with bars and a bad reputation.

"Ladies first," he repeated. "I'm generous with my victims."

Before he could finish, Nia stepped forward — short, fierce, rocking locs and a leather backpack tagged with red, black, and green patches.

She spit fire.

"I don't spit for your weak soul, I spit for the ancestors. For Harriet, for Angela... my speech go! For every girl you tried to silence in the cypher that we know. I write on papyrus and etch glyphs in your ego. You battle to flex — I'm slapping 'em next. I battle to free souls."

The bus crowd erupted.

"YOOOOOO!"

Jamal clapped like a sportscaster.

"She spit that liberation heat!"

Dante pushed up his glasses.

"Rico 'bout to catch a thesis."

Rico didn't grin.

His goons stopped smiling when he glanced at them.

"That was cute," he said. "Now let me show you why Newark makes the best emcees."

He launched into a savage verse — punchlines, venom, style. His delivery slick and brutal. Even Nia tilted her head, acknowledging his flair.

Ty watched quietly.

"First day and we got a revolution and a roast session?"

The bus skidded into the Newark High lot, hydraulic sigh and all.

—

Kids poured off.

Nia tightened her straps.

Ty stepped up.

"Real talk," he said. "That was some heavy bars you were dropping. Never heard a girl spit like that."

"I'm not a girl emcee," she said, stone-faced but cool. "I'm an emcee. Hold that."

She handed him a flyer:

TALENT SHOW – MOVE THE ROOM, SHIFT THE CULTURE

Ty glanced at it, intrigued.

Just then, Rico walked past.

"Nice bars, man," Ty offered.

"Nice bars, man," Rico mocked in a British accent. "Yo, where you from, bruv? Buckingham Palace?"

"Yeah, I'm from—"

"Whatever, England. Stay in your lane, MATE. Don't try and spit here unless you ready to drown."

He brushed past.

Stared Ty down.

Ty stared back.

Unfazed.

"Ooooohhh," Dante called out. "He dubbed you 'England'? That's permanent now, BRUV."

Ty stepped off last.

Flyer in hand.

Backpack tight.

Glow just beneath the surface.

Newark had spoken.

The battle had begun.

—

Newark High loomed ahead — graffiti-tagged, red brick, pulsing with teen energy.

Ty stepped out with a duffel bag and a fresh pair of Clarks Wallabees.

He took a deep breath and stared at the building like it was a new planet.

Another new place.

Another beginning.

—

Boom-bap echoed from someone's headphones.

The hallway smelled like pencil graphite, cologne, and cafeteria fries.

Ty walked with that outsider UK style — alert but cool.

He dodged a paper airplane and adjusted his headphones.

He bumped shoulders with a girl.

She didn't flinch.

Just raised an eyebrow.

"Watch it, London boy…"

He turned.

Afro puffs.

Hoops.

Something in her eyes — like she was watching more than just his face.

"Or maybe you walked into me," he grinned.

She gave the faintest smile.

"Glad you made it your first day…" Then disappeared into a classroom.

Ty kept walking.

—

"Yo England!" a voice called. "That's *Enter the Wu* on your shirt?"

Ty turned.

Jamal — animated, wisecracking — pointed with excitement.

Next to him: Dante — stoic, cool, thick locs, spinning nunchucks by his locker.

"You like Kung Fu?" Dante asked. "Or just the samples?"

"Both," Ty said. "And I do both."

Jamal laughed.

"Ayeee! Finally, somebody who ain't just quoting fight scenes."

They dap up.

The bond was instant.

"Us meeting like this is synchronicity," Jamal said. "We've been looking for an emcee for the talent show. The way you watched that battle on the bus this morning — I had a feeling you might have bars. Spit something. Fulfill the prophecy."

Ty froze for a beat.

Prophecy.

The word hit different.

Then he realized — Jamal didn't know.

It was just a phrase.

"Right here?"

This is what you came to do.

Jamal looked unamused.

"Yes, my brother."

"Some fly Slick Rick style," Dante added.

Ty smirked.

"Nah. I sound like me."

"You sound like something already," Jamal said.

Ty nodded.

"Aight. Check it…"

He bodied the verse.

A freestyle about his journey — from Everlion to Jamaica, from London to Newark.

Pain.

Rhythm.

Legacy.

His voice sharp.

Cadence clean.

Punchlines landing like kicks.

A crowd formed.

Dante recorded, ad-libbing, hyping him up.

Jamal went wild as Ty ended on a punchline synced perfectly with the bell ringing.

Jamal hugged him.

"You came to the right place, Warrior."

Dante uploaded the clip to social media.

They walked down the hallway laughing like they'd known each other for years.

—

Montage – After School

The trio freestyled in the courtyard, beating on benches.

Ty and Dante traded flows for food beneath the bleachers.

Jazz watched from afar.

Calculating.

Knowing.

A quick flash — her eyes glowing faintly in the dark.

—

Jazz's Room – Night

On her desk: a photo of her in Warrior robes, pre-Earth.

A map of Newark pinned to the wall.

Circles.

Strings.

Stars.

He doesn't know it yet... but he brought the war with him.

—

Ty lay in bed.

His phone buzzed.

A text from Dante:

Yo! Your freestyle clip went viral!

Ty sat up.

The dream was moving.

8

Pressure Point Poetry

"The wound of words is worse than the wound of swords." — Arabic Proverb

The parking lot pulsed with bass.

KINZ and WORM walked up to school, nodding hard to a track playing from Kinz's phone. Heads low, eyes locked, they moved like disciples of rhythm.

"Yooo," Kinz said, eyes wide. "This ninja bodied that verse. Pressure point poetry, fam."

"He might be the nicest I heard in a wh—"

"Aye!"

Rico's voice cut through the air like a blade.

"What y'all lookin' at? You on some groupie flex? Gimme that."

He snatched Kinz's phone, rewound the clip, and pressed play.

Ty's freestyle from the hallway played loud.

Rico's jaw tightened.

Behind him, Kinz and Worm reacted again — silent gasps, wide eyes — but kept it cool so Rico wouldn't catch them vibing.

"Nah," Rico muttered. "Hell nah."

He started laughing.

Not joy — something darker.

Joker energy.

"I know this ninja ain't just try to have a BBQ in my backyard and not invite me. I KNOW that's not what's happening right now."

Worm, cautious:

"His name's Ty."

"I ain't ask you his name," Rico snapped. "That's England."

"But you just said—"

"Shut up."

Rico walked off, watching the video again.

His eyes burned with calculation.

Worm leaned in.

"Talent show coming up, my boy. Show heads who's the finest emcee. We know you the illest."

Kinz blinked.

"Aye — that's my phone!"

Rico didn't turn around.

Just kept walking.

Blade flashing briefly under his tongue.

He never acknowledged Kinz.

Never gave the phone back.

—

Next day. Economics class.

Fluorescent hum.

Textbooks open.

Eyes glazed.

Mrs. Beds droned on at the whiteboard.

"If supply increases and demand remains unchanged..."

Ty sat in the back.

Hoodie half-on.

Head tilted.

His desk was a battlefield — scattered notes, doodles, and genius-level graffiti.

He scribbled into his notebook:

Ego too loud for a whisper to guide me. But silence got stories that numbers can't write me.

Next to it, a sketch of a microphone blooming into a sword.

Dante leaned over.

"Yo. That a verse or a weapon?"

Ty smirked.

"Both. Depends who reads it."

Across the room, Jazz watched.

Eyes subtle, but knowing.

She clocked everything — Ty's drawings, his posture, the energy under his stillness.

"He's starting to remember," she whispered to herself.

The bell rang. Chaos.

Backpacks zipped.

Chairs scraped.

Students rushed out like parolees.

Ty stayed seated a moment longer.

They teach us how to buy stock, he thought, *not how to find value. How to take notes, but not how to take notice. So they told us you gotta come with great focus...*

He gently tore out the verse and folded it like a prayer.

—

Hallway. Moments later.

Ty walked slowly while others rushed.

His eyes flicked to Jazz, standing by her locker, observing.

"You always this quiet," she asked, "or just in rooms that make you smaller?"

"Quiet ain't absence," Ty said. "Sometimes it's waiting for the right sound."

She raised an eyebrow, impressed.

"Hmph. Might be louder than you think."

They parted ways.

Something lingered between them.

A looped horn sample played softly in Ty's earbuds — nostalgic, soulful, contemplative.

It felt like memory speaking in jazz.

9

Cracking the Air Open

"When spider webs unite, they can tie up a lion." —
Ethiopian Proverb

Three months later.

Lunch hour faded behind the gym building, where Ty, Jamal, and Dante occupied a quiet corner of the courtyard. A beatbox speaker thumped a looped instrumental — warm, jazzy, eternal.

93 'Til Infinity rode the air like a memory that never aged.

Backpacks sat in a pile.

The trio moved like they'd done this for lifetimes.

"One more run before we hit the show," Jamal said.

"Breathe through your heels," Dante reminded. "Like Sensei said."

"Or just don't choke," Ty added.

Jamal grinned.

"I'm gonna write your name on my mic if I kill it. 'RIP TY: Died of Audacity.'"

They lined up like cipher ninjas.

One beat.

One rhythm.

Ty went first — steady voice, clipped syllables:

"I'm controlling galaxies while ya fallacies are fantasies, My art like galleries — why emcees get burned like calories."

Jamal followed — goofy but sharp:

"Samurai slice with syllables for salaries, The boy been nice — we can skip all formalities."

Then Dante stepped forward.

Slower.

Focused.

Every word sharp like a blade:

"Fists never flinch — fatalities for families, Speak balance now, 'cause war makes for tragedies..."

The beat faded.

They exhaled like they'd just done tai chi.

"Y'all feel that?" Ty asked.

"Yeah," Dante said. "Like we cracked the air open for a second."

"They ain't ready, bro," Jamal said. "We ain't even ready."

They laughed.

But their eyes held something heavier.

They knew this talent show wasn't just a show.

It was a signal.

—

After school.

The trio walked home — backpacks bouncing, mid-debate over lyrics.

"Tell me this line don't hit," Ty said. "'The fire that I spit is dropping heat seekers... I lace the verse like a prophecy's sneakers.'"

"Kinda hard," Jamal said. "If people follow. But my hook got girls and guidance: 'Heart on my sleeve 'til it flex through the pain.'"

"Hooks feed fame," Dante said. "Verses feed souls."

They laughed.

Carefree.

Inspired.

Then the vibe shifted.

Voices echoed from up ahead.

A rival crew leaned against a wall covered in graffiti.

Boombox blasting.

Eyes locked on the trio.

Rico stepped off the curb — sharp fade, icy stare — flanked by Kinz and Worm.

"Ayoooo..." Rico called. "Y'all the ones out here rehearsing school plays and cypher fairytales?"

"It's called preparation, bruh," Jamal said. "Try it sometime."

"Preparation for what?" Kinz added. "Losing?"

"You insecure," Dante asked, "or just volume-challenged?"

Rico stepped in close to Ty.

"This city got teeth, bruv," he said. "And it bites soft-spoken prophets first."

Ty didn't flinch.

"Then I guess it better learn to choke on conviction."

A beat.

Rico smirked.

"Talent show's coming, right? Cool. We'll see who writes truth... or writes excuses."

He flashed a blade from his mouth.

Just a glint.

Just enough.

They backed off.

But the fuse was lit.

Ty watched him walk away.

"Greatness," he said quietly. "They guard the gates from it."

—

That evening, the city pulsed with preparation.

Dante hunched over his notebook — verses pouring like blueprints.

Jamal freestyled in the mirror — charisma sharpening with every line.

Ty moved in silence — his body flowing through martial forms like memory in motion.

Across town, Nia rehearsed — fire in her breath.

Rico's crew plotted, postured, prepared.

Each one shaping their art for battle.

10

The Kick Heard Around the Universe

"The rock in the water does not know the pain of the rock in the sun." - Haitian Proverb

Vinyl Vibrations was more than a job.

It was sanctuary.

The neon sign above the door flickered like it was humming along to the music inside. Sunlight cut through a dusty window, casting golden streaks across rows of vinyl that glistened like sacred archives. A turntable spun something smooth and rootsy — Julian Marley's *Boom Draw* — washing through the air like incense.

Ty moved through the stacks in a faded RUN-DMC tee and fingerless gloves, alphabetizing 45s with care. He hummed along, beatboxed under his breath, fingers dancing like they were tracing rhythm itself.

His eyes lingered on the reggae section — his father's section.

Each record a memory.

He ran his fingers over a familiar cover, the artwork
worn but still vibrant.

*Sometimes I feel like the bassline knows more about
me than I do.*

He dropped the needle on a dub version of Dennis
Brown's *Promised Land.* Closed his eyes. Breathed.
Reset.

Then the chime rang.

A customer entered — tall, bald, dressed in all black,
tinted glasses hiding his eyes. He moved too still.
Browsed slowly. Never flipped a record. Just watched.

Ty glanced up.

Their eyes met.

A chill brushed his neck.

"Need help finding a vibe," Ty asked, half-joking, "or
just waiting to catch one?"

The man smiled.

Thin.

Too slow.

"Just browsing," he said. Then paused. "You ever
feel... like the music's listening to you?"

Ty froze.

The record skipped slightly.

"Yeah," he said. "All the time. Some songs play memories you ain't even lived yet."

The man nodded subtly and turned to leave.

As he passed the security mirror, his reflection glitched — just for a moment.

Obsidian eyes.

Hollowed cheekbones.

A snake-like tongue curled in thought.

Then gone.

The chime rang again.

Ty stood alone.

Silent.

The music distorted for a split second... then corrected.

There's a moment right before a storm, he thought, *where the silence tightens around your ribs. Like truth's trying to whisper, but you're breathing too loud to hear it.*

—

Broad & Market. Night.

The avenue buzzed with corner store neon, teenagers roaming, cops cruising slow.

The air carried equal parts music and menace.

Ty walked alone, headphones on, verses half-whispered under his breath.

Then his ringtone played — a soft piano loop from home. Familiar. His little sister.

He answered.

"Daizja? You good?"

Her voice was shaky.

Distant.

"Ty... he's gone."

"Wait, what? Who?"

"Dad. The news said he robbed a bank. He was running away. Police opened fire. And he's dead. Ty... Dad's gone!"

Ty's knees nearly buckled.

"Dead? And... robbery? What are you saying to me right now? Where's Mum?"

"They said they'd been looking for him for a while. He's gone, Ty. Dad's gone."

Ty stared at a laundromat window.

His reflection blurred in fluorescent flicker.

The music faded.

Silence.

He said the universe paid him back… That lie carried so much love.

—

Later that night.

Ty walked home.

Eyes red.

Shoulders hunched.

He passed a dark alley.

You must conceal your powers in America, Nyah had warned. *Or the Damlyas will find you.*

It's just the universe paying me back, Zorion had said.

Ty imagined them both — crying, distant, fading.

A whistle cut through the air.

Footsteps followed.

Five gang members emerged from the shadows — bandanas, brass knuckles, joking like jackals.

"Ayoooooo," the leader called. "Where you goin' with that sad poet posture, London?"

"This ain't the night, bruv," Ty said.

"Ain't never the night. 'Til it is."

They circled him.

Ty's fists tightened.

Grief shifted into quiet fire.

He didn't fall, Ty whispered to himself. *He flew... through fire for me.*

The first punch landed.

Then another.

Ty dropped — not because they had him.

He wanted to feel the pain.

He rose slowly.

Wiped blood from his lip.

Bruce Lee style.

Then he shifted.

Fighting stance.

Glow rising.

Bruce LeRoy energy.

Time slowed.

A gold tear slid down Ty's cheek.

His eyes lit up.

One gang member lunged.

Ty dodged — impossibly fast — and countered with an open-palm strike that sent the guy flying into a dumpster.

The others rushed.

Ty moved like he'd been doing this in dreams.

Fluid martial forms.

Sparks erupted with each blow.

One thug swung a bat — Ty caught it mid-air and shattered it with a pulse from his palm.

Final move:

Ty launched mid-air.

Kicked one in the chest.

Sent him flying across a stair rail.

His yell carried everything — grief, rage, legacy.

"WAAAAHDAHHHHH!"

Lightning surrounded the kick.

It was the signal.

The one the Damlyas had been waiting for.

Ty landed.

Hoodie torn.

Eyes glowing.

He knew.

I guess there's no avoiding your destiny.

Silence.

Bodies groaned around him.

A passerby peeked from a window, terrified.

Ty stood in the alley.

Not proud.

Not angry.

Just awake.

Sometimes you don't step into your destiny, he thought. *Sometimes it crashes into your ribs... and asks if you're ready to breathe different.*

11

The Chune of Your Soul

"When the mind is still, the universe surrenders." —
Indian Proverb

Moonlight crept through the blinds, striping the room in silver.

Shadows stretched across the walls like quiet memories.

Ty lay on his back, fully clothed, hands laced on his chest.

Eyes wide open.

Still.

The TV glowed mute.

An old kung fu flick played — Shaolin monks flipping through air in slow motion.

But Ty wasn't watching.

He turned slowly, opened the drawer beside him, and pulled out an old photo album.

The edges were worn.

The tape yellowing.

He flipped through the pages.

Ty at age five, squinting into the sun on the coast.

Zorion behind him, early thirties, showing him a stance — knees bent, open palms up.

—

They stood barefoot on soft dirt.

"The body listens better when the soul leads," Zorion said.

"But my legs itch," young Ty complained.

Zorion laughed.

"Good. That's power waking up."

He adjusted Ty's arms, showed him how to breathe with his belly.

The wind rustled the trees, and somewhere, faintly, a golden shimmer of light followed the motion of their movements.

"One day," Zorion said, "the fire in you will try to run wild. Don't fear it. Dance with it."

—

Back in his room, Ty brushed away a single tear.

Then flipped the page.

Final photo: his father and mother holding him, wrapped in gold cloth.

He stared at it for a long time.

"I get it now," he whispered. "You didn't die... You transferred."

He closed the album like a spell.

"And the rest... I'll carry."

—

The next day.

Ty met Jazz at a forgotten basketball court tucked between rusted fences and cracked pavement.

The hoop had no net.

Spray tags bled into brick.

The court wasn't in good condition.

Now it was a dojo.

They stood barefoot in the center, sun slicing through clouds overhead.

Their breathing matched.

Postures loose, then precise.

They moved through forms:

Palms slicing the air in perfect rhythm.

Steps patterned around an invisible spiral.

Hands glowing faintly at the fingertips — just a shimmer.

"Your flow's off-center," Jazz said. "You're thinking."

"I got a right to think," Ty replied. "The sky's about to break open and drop darkness."

She sighed.

Rolled her shoulders.

Stepped forward.

"You're not wrong to fear it. You'd be a fool if you didn't."

"Then what's this all for?" Ty asked. "Us swinging our hands in corners no one walks down."

She threw a palm at his chest.

He blocked — late.

"It's not about the technique," she said. "It's the tune."

"The what?"

"The tune of your soul. The thing the Damlyas can't imitate. You've been rhyming it since birth... you just didn't know what you were scoring."

She stepped closer.

"You possess the inner power to bring life, color, and beauty to all things. If your energy multiplies, it could destroy every Damlya. But more than that — it could awaken others. Help them realize their own greatness. That's the real threat."

Ty slowed.

Dropped his shoulders.

Closed his eyes.

He moved — not with steps, but with memory.

Each stance recalled the teachings of his father, the pull of ancient instinct.

The dust around his feet swirled into a perfect circle.

His hands glowed subtly.

He opened his eyes.

"You think the prophecy's real?"

"I think truth doesn't need belief to become itself."

She paused.

"And you? You're what happens when past, present, and purpose stop fighting each other."

She extended a hand.

He gripped it.

"My parents didn't send me here for music," Ty said. "They sent me to get away from the Damlyas."

Jazz nodded.

"And now the inevitable time seems near. They've destroyed entire planets. Now they've come here — for you. Or they'll destroy Earth."

Ty looked on.

Brave.

"Do I sense fear in you?" she asked.

"I used to think fear was weakness," Ty said. "But now... I think it's just energy. Waiting to be shaped."

"But shaped into what?"

They didn't answer.

They moved.

Two silhouettes spinning in motion.

Arms sweeping skyward.

On a cracked court, with crumbling fences, the dance of legacy began again.

12

What You Do After Fear Speaks

"The longest journey you will make in your life is from your head to your heart." - Native American Proverb

Jazz's hideout was part dojo, part war room, part vinyl dream.

A converted underground mechanic shop turned apartment, it hummed with low-frequency tech and the scent of sandalwood. Shadows clung to the corners like secrets.

The walls told stories:

- Wall one: rusted shelves of nunchaku, spears, and bladed fans.

- Wall two: illuminated holographic star maps, strange glyphs pulsing like breathing constellations.

- Wall three: framed posters — Bruce Lee, Grace Jones, Haile Selassie, MF DOOM — watching like ancestors.

At the center, a circular mat glowed faintly with alien markings.

Ty stepped in, wide-eyed but silent.

"You training warriors," he asked, "or building a vinyl cover?"

Jazz didn't look up.

"Both. It's the same thing if you're doing it right."

She knelt before the mat and pressed her palm to the center disk.

A golden constellation pulsed upward — Everlion connected to Earth via ancient corridors.

"Your father... your mother... weren't just hiding from war," she said. "They were hiding you from prophecy."

"Because of what I might become?"

"No," she said. "Because of what you'd have to survive to become it."

She tossed a file folder toward him.

Inside: surveillance images. Static. Glowing signatures. Damlya shapeshifters dissolving into mist outside places Ty had lived — London. Jamaica. Newark.

"They've been watching you for years," Jazz said. "And then? You lit up like a flare in the astral grid."

Ty stared at the images.

His jaw tightened.

"So we wait here? Or we hit back?"

Jazz smiled.

Sharp.

Proud.

"We start shaping your mind like a blade. And when they come? You won't be a target. You'll be a mirror — showing them what they fear most."

—

Training began.

No montage.

Just rhythm.

Ty and Jazz sparred hand-to-hand, their movements blending Earth martial forms with alien gravity-bending sweeps.

Each strike hummed with intention.

Each block echoed with memory.

Ty repeated a movement.

Again.

Again.

His eyes glowed slightly brighter with each pass.

Jazz taught him to slow his thoughts until time nearly froze.

To breathe from the belly.

To listen with the bones.

He levitated small objects between his palms without realizing.

Sweat dripped.

Muscles burned.

The air around them shimmered.

"If I'm supposed to be chosen," Ty said, catching his breath, "why does it still feel like I'm guessing?"

Jazz paused.

"Because humility's the lock," she said. "Power's just the key. And greatness? That lives in what you do after fear finishes speaking."

Ty nodded.

Quiet.

Focused.

He stepped toward the mirror.

His reflection stared back — half his face, familiar.

The other half, translucent, golden, glowing with ancient lineage.

He didn't flinch.

He just looked.

13

Try Me in Stereo

"The lion does not turn around when a small dog barks."
— Yoruba Proverb

Vinyl Vibrations pulsed with low bass and quiet memory.

Ty leaned behind the counter, pretending to read liner notes but clearly zoned out.

His eyes glazed.

Mind elsewhere.

When the world flips, he thought, *the silence after ain't peace. It's pressure.*

The bell over the door jingled.

Sakira walked in — green hoodie, headphones around her neck, honey in her steps.

Ty perked up without meaning to.

"Look who finally made it up to see me again," he said.

She glanced at his hand on the records.

"You filing that under 'W' for 'Whatever,' or you just alphabetically rebellious?"

"This?" Ty said. "It's under 'S' for 'Still Thinkin' Bout You." He paused. "In a cool, non-creepy way."

She laughed and leaned on the counter.

A soft moment.

Familiar.

Almost warm.

Then the door slammed open.

Rico and his crew strode in — laughing loud, dragging the energy down like static in a groove.

"Ah, the poet with a punch," Rico said. "Shakespeare, you work retail now? Haha."

"Yeah," Ty replied. "Helps me budget out how many syllables it'll take to silence you."

"Ooooh," Kinz smirked. "He talkin' like a mixtape again."

Tension crackled.

Sakira stood between them, unimpressed.

"Y'all make entrances like sitcoms," she said, "but leave like extras. What's the point?"

Rico stared at Ty.

Then nodded.

And exited.

Almost too easy.

Then the door opened again.

The mysterious customer from before walked in —
slow, deliberate, dark shades.

Same presence.

But now?

Ty was ready.

"I know who you are," he said.

The man smiled.

Calm.

"Then you know I could've ended this... a long time
ago."

"Yeah," Ty said. "But now you're standing in a store
with twelve cameras, two martial artists on speed dial...
and a kid who just realized fear's bad at math."

The man removed his glasses.

His eyes shifted to black.

Slitted pupils.

Skin rippled.

They moved.

—

The Damlya scout lunged — slashing Ty across the chest.

His shirt ripped.

Blood bloomed.

Sakira didn't hesitate.

She moved with him.

The record shop became a battlefield.

Classic hip-hop and reggae records flew like ninja stars.

Shelves exploded.

Beats thumped.

Vinyls sliced through air like blades.

Ty pivoted off walls, dodged shadow tendrils.

He channeled breath.

His hands radiated light.

A palm strike blasted the Damlya into a speaker stack.

The scout rose — snarling, hissing in another language.

"You want prophecy?" Ty said, low. "Try me in stereo."

He screamed.

Energy crackled.

Burst outward.

Windows shattered — outward, not inward.

The Damlya flickered.

Growled.

Then retreated into smoke.

—

Ty stood in the center of shattered vinyls.

Breathing hard.

Sakira stared at him.

Eyes wide.

But not afraid.

"You always been this... different?" she asked softly.

"Yeah," Ty said. "I just didn't know it had a name."

—

Sometimes the first battle you win, Ty thought, *is the moment you stop hiding from it.*

14

The Beat That Built It

"Every hoe ha dem stick a bush." - Jamaican Proverb

Newark exhaled steam and solitude.

Ty walked Sakira to her car, the streetlamp casting long shadows behind them. Her voice trembled, but her stance stayed strong.

"I need you to explain to me what that thing was," she said. "What is going on? Who are you?"

"I'll explain everything," Ty said. "I promise. But right now, you gotta get out of here."

He handed her a spare key.

"You should stay at mine. I'm laying low until I figure out what that guy was... and if he's coming back with reinforcements."

Sakira shook her head.

"I couldn't if I wanted to. I've got kids depending on me — donations to deliver tomorrow morning. I can't let them down."

She paused.

"But I trust you. I always knew there was something different about you. I just... knew."

Ty nodded.

"Thanks for coming up. Sorry it had to be like this. Thanks for being here for me — from UK to US. Not being too weirded out means a lot."

"Finding out your childhood friend is part of the intergalactic federation?" she said. "Everyday stuff, really. No biggie."

They laughed.

Then quieted.

"I'll call you when I get home," she said.

"Stay safe," Ty replied. "Head on a swivel, yeah?"

They embraced.

A caring gaze.

Then she was gone.

—

From across the street, Jazz watched Sakira drive off.

Her eyes held curiosity.

Maybe jealousy.

Maybe something deeper.

Ty walked back toward the store.

Jazz met him halfway.

They walked together under the warm buzz of street lamps.

Shop signs hummed neon.

Alley murals glowed — Afrofuturist phoenixes, faded Big L quotes, hands drawn holding constellations.

"You really cracked his ribs with that chi push?" Jazz asked.

"He had it comin'," Ty said. "Might've loosened a few of my own with the landing, though."

"Grace takes time," she said. "Still... I felt that wave from a few blocks away. Like something real opened in you."

A kid rolled past on a BMX, headphones on.

The beat seeped into the sidewalk.

"I been walking like I was just visiting this life," Ty said. "Now I feel like my body's not a hiding spot. It's a drum."

"A drum?"

"Yeah. Like something ancient's playing through me. Like... the rhythm ain't new. I'm just finally tuned to it."

He paused.

"I thought I was scared of dying. But it was deserving this that had me duckin'."

They stopped at a fire escape ladder.

Exchanged a look.

"Ready?" Jazz asked.

Ty didn't answer.

He just climbed.

—

The rooftop opened into sky and steel.

Wind brushed their faces.

Above: stars.

Below: a sleeping city waiting on its champion.

Jazz stepped back.

"This rooftop's yours," she said.

Ty exhaled.

Closed his eyes.

His heartbeat slowed.

Then doubled.

Then warped into a bass drum.

His veins glowed golden.

His shoes lifted a centimeter off the concrete.

He blinked — suddenly behind her.

Then beside her.

Then back again.

Super speed.

He laughed softly.

"Whaaat..."

He slammed his palm into the ground.

The rooftop cracked beneath it.

A passing bird startled.

Ty gasped — and vanished.

Invisibility.

Then he rematerialized, hovering three feet in the air.

He closed his fists.

Golden claws emerged, humming with energy.

He curled them back in, breathing hard.

His hands sparked.

Tiny pulsing orbs formed between his fingers.

He aimed at the air — and blasted a pure beam of light across the cityscape.

It hit a water tower miles away with a silent burst of gold.

Jazz stared.

Awestruck.

"You're not learning your power," she said. "You're remembering it."

Ty nodded.

"When I was in that last street fight," he said, "something clicked. I understood all at once what my father had been trying to teach me."

He looked out over the city.

"I had to remember the feeling of the wish fulfilled — for these powers to come to life. I had to be. I had to assume I was already what I thought I might become."

He turned to her.

"In those fights... it's like I was only acting on my clearest thoughts and deepest feelings. Then expressing myself. And that — that's when my powers came."

He raised his hands.

"The power comes from me believing in myself. My own raw self-expression. The artist within me. My own greatness. And when I assume the greatness in me is unlimited... well then, so am I."

"This ain't just in my blood," he said. "It's who I am."

"It's in every time you didn't quit," Jazz said. "Every rhyme you ever wrote. Every breath your father left behind."

Ty touched his temple.

His eyes widened.

"I hear you," he said. "You're not saying it out loud... but I hear you."

Jazz grinned.

"Telepathy's cute. I've had it since twelve."

"You could've warned me about the claws."

They stepped to the edge together.

The city sparkled below.

"This isn't about me saving the world," Ty said quietly. "It's about protecting the beat that built it."

"And we protect it," Jazz said, "by becoming the sound it needs."

She paused.

"You're not becoming the prophecy. You're becoming someone who could rewrite it."

The wind curled around them like a tide waiting to rise.

Ty raised one hand.

A sphere of light spun in his palm.

Not exploding.

Just pulsing.

Like breath.

15

Rhythm and Ruin

"If you do not know where you are going, any road will take you there." — Akan Proverb

Jamaica, Years Ago

The morning bloomed with color and sound.

Children chased kites made from coconut shells. A rasta stirred peanut porridge while humming. Goats wandered lazily past a dominoes match. Reggae poured from a distant transistor radio. Somewhere nearby, a grandmother fried festival while Beres Hammond played low and sweet.

The breeze carried laughter, spice, and rhythm.

Beyond the bustle, behind tall sugarcane, a hidden grove waited.

In the center of the clearing, young Zorion stood barefoot in a deep stance. Shirtless. Eyes shut. Focused. Tiny freckles of light shimmered around his palms.

Novi moved slowly in front of him — radiant, calm, her body flowing like water. She demonstrated a sequence, fluid and deliberate, almost like dance.

"Every breath is a blade," she said. "Every silence, a shield. Let the world pass by... but don't let it pass through you."

Zorion opened his eyes. Mimicked the movement. Too fast. He stumbled.

"But why hide it," he asked, "if we're strong enough to stop them?"

"Because strength shown too soon becomes invitation," Novi said, kneeling before him. "Not protection."

Her eyes were soft, yet piercing.

"This land sings in peace. Your power... must whisper with it."

Zorion tried again. Slower. His hands flowed in rhythm with the wind. A nearby mango fell — but landed gently, caught midair by invisible force.

He smiled.

"Now again," Novi said. "But this time, let the sky guide your foot... not your fear."

—

They called it **Silent Sundays**.

Novi and Zorion sat at the edge of a cliff, listening to ocean waves. She taught him how to sync his breath with bird calls. They sipped sorrel in silence. Sparred under full moons. Every motion tight and quiet.

Zorion's powers — flight, telekinesis, subtle glows — were present. But always held back. Not shown.

Back in the grove, Zorion asked:

"Do you think they'll ever find us?"

"The Damlyas are not the only danger," Novi said. "Fear can do worse. It can turn you against yourself."

She wiped sweat from his forehead. Smiled.

"That's why you train, little one. So when they come... you'll know when to disappear. And when not to."

They bowed to each other in a final stance.

The sun dipped between palms.

The sugarcane waved.

This was the boy who would one day save his son — by teaching him how to listen first, and strike later.

Everlion, Present

Obsidian clouds rippled across the sky, glowing faintly like bruises in twilight.

Lightning danced behind clawed towers that jutted into space like weapons carved by regret.

The Damlya army knelt in solemn fractals — silent, armor slick with memory.

The wind didn't howl.

It waited.

Ancient glyphs pulsed across the cliffs — scripture etched in bone and fire.

A mural carved into obsidian showed Vorrak's rise: not born, but assembled. A child of war, stitched from the memories of fallen prophets. His heart forged in the Crucible of Silence, where screams were currency and mercy extinct.

From the soul-forged throne, Vorrak rose.

He didn't walk.

He unfolded — like a verdict.

His crown writhed like nerve endings.

His voice didn't echo.

It burrowed.

"This place..." Vorrak said. "This planet of art, heart, rhythm and rebellion... Earth is a thief of silence. It births music from pain. Art from poverty. Light from rot. Their melodies infect the void. Their images dare to heal."

He stepped forward.

"And one child, born of prophecy and rhythm, threatens legacy. Ty."

He raised a soul-glass sphere.

Inside, the last flicker of Zorion's defiance faded.

"His father bought his son's escape with stolen coin and fading hope. But Earth never arrested him. We did. Disguised as their police. Wrapped in their trust. And when he surrendered to their authority... he surrendered to us."

South London, Eight Months Ago

Rain fell like needles.

The alley was a coffin of shadows.

Zorion ran. Desperate. Behind him, sirens screamed. Police lights flickered.

Two uniformed officers stepped forward. Calm. Reassuring.

Zorion exhaled. Ready to surrender.

Then the world glitched.

Badges melted into black sludge.

Skin split like rotten fruit.

Eyes blazed neon red.

Mouths stretched too wide.

The Damlyas revealed themselves — inhuman, twitching, whispering in a language that made the walls bleed.

The air bent.

Vorrak arrived.

Not with sound, but subtraction.

Color drained.

Time stuttered.

Even memory recoiled.

He descended last — levitating, cloaked in smoke and bone, his face a shifting void.

A dozen surrounded Zorion.

He fought like a man possessed.

Fists flying.

Heart roaring.

But the Damlyas didn't bleed.

They laughed in reverse.

Moved like broken time — jerking, phasing, multiplying.

The alley sealed shut.

No escape.

No sound.

Just the hiss of reality unraveling.

Vorrak raised a mirror-blade.

Its surface shimmered with Zorion's worst imagined memories — his daughter crying, his wife praying, Ty trapped.

"You gave him spirit," Vorrak said. "I give you silence... and suffering."

The blade pierced Zorion's chest.

Didn't kill him.

It rooted into him.

His veins turned black.

His eyes rolled back.

He screamed — but the Damlyas stole the sound.

Bottled it.

Drank it.

They reached inside him — not physically, but spiritually.

Ripped out his memories, one by one.

Each became a living echo — his daughter's voice, his mother's lullaby — twisted, mocked, played back in demonic tones.

Zorion watched his life burn backwards.

He begged for death.

Vorrak denied it.

Finally, the Damlyas carved his soul from his body and hung it in the air — a glowing, screaming orb.

They shattered it.

The alley went dark.

Zorion's body dropped.

Empty.

Hollow.

Forgotten.

Only a smear of blood remained.

And a whisper that cursed the wind.

Everlion, Present

Vorrak turned to the kneeling army.

"You call me warlord. Prophet. Monster. But I am the answer to your prayers."

He raised his arms.

"You begged for order. I gave you silence. You begged for truth. I gave you extinction."

"Earth will not be conquered. It will be cleansed."

Behind him, the gate split reality open — black flame twisting toward Earth.

In the war crucible, Vorrak stood alone.

Before him, a swirling map of Earth rotated in crimson mist.

A faint image of Azariah flickered in the smoke — defiant even in memory.

"Your blood scattered light into the void," Vorrak whispered. "But light... always returns home."

He smashed the map.

Sparks scattered like stars.

"They will call me tyrant," he said. "But history will call me necessary. And when the last rhythm fades..."

He turned.

"Only my silence will remain."

The cosmic gate bloomed behind him.

The invasion had begun.

16

Pages of the Same Verse

"The soul would have no rainbow if the eyes had no tears." - Cherokee Proverb

Soft light spilled through the blinds.

A kettle whistled somewhere in the distance.

Books were stacked like constellations.

The scent of old vinyl and possibility hung in the air.

Hip-hop hummed low from the radio — something thoughtful, Dilla-esque.

Cracked records still littered the floor from yesterday's battle.

Ty entered with Jazz.

Both visibly shaken.

Both trying not to show it.

Sakira stood in the kitchen, sipping something hot like she owned the lease.

"Well look who stumbled in like they just outran a ghost with a gym membership," she said. "Y'all good, or should I start prepping the obits?"

Ty didn't answer.

Just dropped the keys.

Jazz spoke, direct.

"That quiet customer at the shop? Not human. He was a Damlya scout."

Sakira's smirk dissolved.

She stepped back, but didn't look away.

"And what specifically is a Damlya," she asked, "and why were they in Newark?"

Ty chuckled dryly.

Then straightened.

His shirt was fresh, but the bandage beneath it peeked through.

He sat down at the dining table.

Across from him, Sakira — calm, collected, rocking a denim jacket and a look that searched deeper than words.

"Didn't mean to dip so quick last night," she said. "But you know I fight for the kids."

Ty nodded.

"No worries."

She sat across from him.

A quiet settled between them.

One of weight and waiting.

"I owe you answers," Ty said. "Real ones."

"I'm listening," Sakira replied, leaning in.

Ty took a breath.

Deeper than most.

Like he was pulling memory up from muscle.

"There's an alien species," he said. "Damlyas. Cold-blooded soul-killers. They conquer galaxies... but not with armies. With silence. With control. No rhythm. No art. No joy."

"They came for Earth," he continued, "because this planet pulses different. Because people here make music that shakes dimensions."

Sakira's voice softened.

"And you?"

"I'm what they fear most. A glitch. My grandfather was one of them. My grandmother was a Warrior of Light. And I was born on Earth. Three bloodlines. One beat."

He opened a worn leather pouch.

Inside: a glowing scroll.

He unrolled it gently.

Glyphs shifted like liquid light across its surface.

"Everything my pops taught me — kung fu, breathwork, discipline — wasn't just training. It was preparation. The prophecy didn't land on him. It landed in me."

"So that... glow?" Sakira asked. "At the pitch? In the store?"

"First flare," Ty said. "Each time I step into truth, it pulses stronger. They feel it. Across the stars."

She touched the scroll.

Her fingers sparked faintly.

Ty noticed.

She pulled back, unsure.

"You got soul, Sakira," he said. "Real rhythm. They'll feel you too if we're not careful."

Outside: sirens passed.

Inside: silence returned.

"I would say this is hard to believe," Sakira said, "but I always knew you were different. But why me? What made you get close to me?"

"Because you never looked away," Ty said. "Not from me. Not from my madness. And now I need someone who can help me stay grounded... as the world flips."

She stood slowly.

Paced once.

Then turned.

"Then tell me how to fight," she said. "Because I don't do sidelines."

Ty grinned, just slightly.

The scroll pulsed brighter.

Some people hear your rhythm, he thought. *Some people move with it. But the ones who hold it with you? That's family.*

Jazz pulled a triangular device from her coat.

Set it on the table.

It flickered to life — holographic lines traced Newark.

Points of red started blinking inward.

"They're coordinated," Jazz said. "Not local crews. Not random violence. This ain't pressure. It's procedure. Forty-eight hours. Maybe less."

Sakira stared at the map.

Then at Ty.

"Guess this means we stop waiting on the storm," she said. "And start building the levees."

Ty looked at her.

Finally seeing she wasn't just part of this.

She was ready for it.

"Then we start tonight," he said. "There are Warriors of Light Ascendants my parents always said would help me when the time came. We find them. Bring 'em in."

He stood.

"When the fight comes, we're gonna be ready. If Newark is gonna make me... then it's gonna rise with me too."

The table glowed brighter.

Points aligning.

Ty, Sakira, and Jazz — each caught in the light like pages of the same verse.

Not chosen by fate.

Choosing each other.

17

Wings and Beacons

"When the character of a man is not clear to you, look at his friends." — Japanese Proverb

England, Years Ago

Steam rose in the industrial kitchen.

Fluorescent lights buzzed overhead like tired thoughts.

Zorion wiped sweat from his brow with a different rag than the one he'd just used to clean the counter.

His apron was stained.

His posture proud, but tired.

He moved like a warrior holding invisible weight.

"You're still on shift?" a co-worker called. "That's sixteen hours, mate."

Zorion smiled faintly.

"Dreams don't clock out."

—

Later, on the public bus, Zorion sat with eyes half-closed.

Outside, the cold steel of London passed: dim flats, blurred graffiti, chain-link fences.

He clutched a worn photo of Ty at age six, holding a toy microphone.

There was a smile in that photo Zorion hadn't seen in years.

—

In a stockroom under a flickering bulb, Zorion stacked boxes.

His left shoulder pulsed from years of quiet injuries.

He set a box down.

Breathed hard.

He closed his eyes.

Flashes returned: young Ty laughing as they shared fish and chips. Novi stirring fish tea in a red clay pot. Warm sun.

No silence like this.

Then back to cold brick.

Humming generator.

—

Early morning.

The door creaked open.

Zorion stepped into a cramped flat.

Peeled off gloves.

Set down his coat.

A pile of letters on the table: "Past Due." "Final Notice."

He ignored them.

Walked past.

Entered the tiny bedroom where Ty slept.

Ty stirred slightly.

Zorion knelt beside the bed.

Stared at his son.

Whispered — not to Ty, but to the night.

"Maybe I couldn't give you the sky," he said. "But I swear... every brick I laid was to help you build wings."

From the window, snow began to fall.

Inside, Zorion stood with his head resting against the glass.

The warmth of Jamaica was long gone.

But love?

Love glowed, even in the cold.

Newark, Present Day

The rooftop glimmered with neon reflections.

Car horns echoed like fading questions.

Ty, Sakira, and Jazz stood in a triangle.

A portable holo-projector glowed at their feet, spinning a rotating map of Earth.

Pulses of light blinked across continents.

"You saying these ain't guesses?" Ty asked. "These dots… they're actual people?"

"Not people," Jazz said. "Frequencies. Some dormant. Some flaring up. But they're real. Warriors like us. Some forgotten. Some not awakened yet."

Sakira stared at the dot flashing in Egypt.

Another glowed in Ghana.

One blinked softly in Newark.

"So what," she said, "this is gonna be like the Avengers — but broke and bilingual?"

Ty smirked.

"Avengers don't have verses. What's Hulk saying to me in a rap battle?"

Sakira grinned faintly.

"Even when the stakes is high, you got jokes."

They laughed.

Briefly.

But the urgency settled in again like fog.

"We'll need couriers," Jazz said. "Dreamwalkers. Those who still move between realms. I know a healer in Lagos who can patch a soul with sound... and an old warrior in Seoul who trains from midnight to dawn."

"What if they won't join us?" Ty asked.

"Then we show 'em why they woke up glowing," Sakira said. "Remind 'em: this fight chose them because they're the light."

Ty stepped toward the edge of the roof.

The wind kicked up.

His energy hummed — gentle but present.

"We don't need a thousand warriors," he said. "Just the right few. The ones who ain't scared to speak with their whole chest. The ones who remember what love costs."

He paused.

"If the Damlyas wanna take this world… they better bring earplugs. Because we're gonna make so much noise… the universe gon' get jealous."

They placed their fists together over the glowing map.

Three pulses synced.

One Newark spark.

One spirit.

From above, the rooftop glowed — then shot a beacon into the sky, unseen by most.

Across the map, dots flickered.

One by one, they began to shine.

The call had been made.

18

One Beat, Three Directions

"A river that forgets its source will dry up." - Nigerian Proverb

The apartment was dimly lit.

Records stacked like altars.

Maps sprawled across the floor.

Incense curled in the air like spirit smoke.

Ty, Sakira, and Jazz sat in a loose triangle.

The only light came from the alien projector pulsing over the coffee table — a globe rotating in soft golds, bright spots flickering like prayers trying to become people.

Ty stared at North America.

Jazz eyed Africa.

Sakira scrolled through South America on a battered tablet, sipping matcha.

"Africa's flaring up like a drum circle with something to prove," Jazz said. "Old rhythms waking up. I can feel 'em vibrating through the floor."

"North America's got one signal," Ty said. "Newark. Strong. Steady. Feels like a warrior with headphones on and zero time for small talk."

Sakira flipped the tablet toward them.

A blinking light pulsed near the Andes.

"I got one in the jungle outside Medellín," she said. "Either a light being or somebody really committed to becoming one with their ayahuasca trip."

They chuckled.

Jazz logged notes.

Ty kept staring at the map.

"So we split?" he asked. "Three continents. Three of us. I don't like it."

"You don't have to like it," Jazz said. "You just have to trust it."

Sakira's voice softened.

"That's the real war, isn't it? Trust. The missions are easy. It's the waiting on someone else to come back breathing that's hard."

Ty picked up the crystal core from the projector.

It glowed in his hand, reacting to him.

He frowned.

"Why does it always do that when I touch it? Feels like it's reading my chakras and judging me."

"Maybe it knows you tried to microwave a Pop-Tart with the foil on last month," Sakira said.

"You need to let that go," Ty replied. "That was a science experiment."

Jazz smirked, already packing gear.

Ty stood and started gathering folded maps, marking routes with neon tape.

His voice was calmer now.

Commanding, but soft.

"We each take a piece of Earth's rhythm. South America. Africa. North America. You feel something shift? You call. You don't show up? We find you anyway."

Jazz looked up.

"You finally sound like a leader."

Ty paused.

"Nah. I just sound like somebody who's ready to own what I feel."

—

As they packed, the projector flickered.

Sakira saw her reflection in the glass.

The glow from the core pulsed oddly near her.

She hesitated.

Her hand lingered an extra second.

"You good?" Ty asked.

She snapped out of it.

"Yeah. Just... thinking about how we all started this with one truth. And now we're carrying enough secrets to build a tomb."

Jazz looked at her.

Not suspicious.

But present.

"Secrets are only deadly if they stay locked too long," she said.

They each rested one hand on the glowing core.

It responded — humming, syncing with their breath.

"This ain't about being the strongest," Ty said. "This is about being found. By rhythm. By spirit. By each other."

They nodded.

Ty closed the map.

The apartment dimmed.

One pulse remained in the center of the table.

Three signals echoing outward.

They exited separately.

Sakira's glance back lingered.

One last look.

Like she was memorizing them.

Or already mourning them.

19

The Ones Who Sharpen the Blade

"A warrior is not one who fights, but one who protects." - Tanzanian Proverb

Newark – Present Day

Sun popped off double-dutch ropes.

Pop-up tents lined the sidewalks.

Vinyl stalls.

Roti steam.

Murals breathing in color.

Ty walked it all like rhythm — head up, hoodie down.

This was the Newark that raised him.

Rebuilt him.

A group of bike kids wheeled past, loud.

"Yo Ty!" one shouted. "You still owe us that cafeteria freestyle, bro!"

Ty grinned.

"Y'all want bars or bedtime stories? Pick one!"

—

Outside a bodega, Raheem and Tanya posted up with drinks and opinions.

"Lemme guess," Raheem said. "You signing to Def Jam and 'bout to dip again?"

"Nah," Ty replied. "I'm here to make sure I do my part to be a part of the community."

"Mmhmm," Tanya said. "That what this glow-up's about? Cosmic messiah vibes with a side of Newark guilt?"

They dapped.

There was love.

But there was realness too.

"Rico been circlin'," Raheem said. "Quiet lately, but loud in the way trouble whispers. You see him, remember — he still think this city owes him tribute."

Ty nodded.

Didn't flinch.

—

The block party bloomed in the school parking lot.

The DJ spun throwback bangers.

"La Schmoove" warped into "Murder She Wrote."

Dominoes cracked.

Aunties danced with fans like flags.

Banners flapped: *Neighborhood Clean-Up.*

Ty strolled in.

Shoulder taps.

Nods.

Hugs.

But his eyes stayed alert.

Near the makeshift bar — Rico.

Gold rope chain.

Sweat-slick arrogance.

Looking like a statue of someone who never got the statue.

Their eyes locked.

Rico pounced.

"Word is you been floating through town like Newark's spirit guide," he said. "Or ghost. Can't tell which."

"Just movin'," Ty said calmly. "Old street. New rhythm."

"Funny," Rico snorted. "Rhythm got you talkin' soft these days. Used to be, you spit, people stood back."

"Now I spit and people wake up," Ty said. "There's a difference between shaking the room... and shifting the ground."

Rico stepped closer.

Crowd leaned in.

One push.

Just pressure.

Ty exhaled.

Didn't step back.

Didn't rise.

Just was.

"Real power don't flex," he said. "It just doesn't flinch."

Rico lunged.

Two OGs stepped in fast — Mr. Will and Auntie Nene, slick with wisdom and cologne.

"This block built bars," Mr. Will said. "Not battlefields."

"You wanna fight," Auntie Nene added, "take it to a beat. Otherwise? Sit down or sit out."

Rico backed off.

Ego bruised but performative.

"See you at the talent show, bruv," he yelled over the crowd.

The party moved on like it never happened.

—

Ty moved through the crowd, gathering intel.

A vinyl vendor whispered about a woman in Chicago whose voice made the mic levitate.

A little girl chalked glowing hands on the ground.

When Ty knelt down, she said:

"I saw them in my dream."

A Brazilian dancer leaned in near the speaker tent.

"In Rio... a favela lit up last week. Not guns. Light. Big. Silent. Beautiful."

Ty walked alone near the edge of the street.

Palmed an energy crystal.

It flickered once.

Twice.

Then pulsed — west.

"That's another one," he whispered.

Jamaica – Years Ago

Cicadas sang between breaths.

Bamboo swayed like memory.

Zorion walked beside Novi — regal and radiant in her calm.

Her Earth form was weather-worn but glowing.

He carried only a satchel and too many regrets.

Locals greeted them softly.

A wrinkled elder pressed warm sweetbread into Zorion's hand.

"No need fi prove nothin' here," Novi said, her voice laced with Patois. "Yuh presence is enough. Peace first... then breath. Then battle, if necessary."

Zorion nodded.

Didn't speak.

—

Later that night, the moon cast long shadows across a patch of earth ringed with torches.

Novi moved through slow, deliberate stances — ancient kung fu encoded with memory.

Zorion imitated.

Too tense.

His form collapsed.

He growled, frustrated, and punched the dirt.

"I studied. I trained. I bled with belief in a future that was mine."

"You loved the prophecy," Novi said. "But didn't listen to its pacing."

She knelt beside him.

Palmed the hilt of his spirit staff.

"Some of us born to lift the blade," she said. "Others... are born to sharpen it."

—

Children gathered with torches, mimicking Novi's stances.

Giggling until she hushed them with a wink.

Zorion drew constellations in the dirt, linking them to glyphs from Everlion.

Novi and a village drummer chanted in harmony.

Vibrations rose around them.

A stone mural was painted slowly — a glowing figure holding Earth in careful balance.

—

In a bamboo shelter deep in the night, Novi and Zorion sat beneath woven netting.

Candlelight cast runes on their faces.

Zorion sharpened a carved spear that hummed when near fire.

"Something's shifting," he said. "Like the stars... forgot their pattern. You feel it, don't you?"

Novi didn't open her eyes.

But she heard everything.

"They are not chasing us, son," she said. "They're hunting rhythm. Following pulse like scent... But what waits for them... is not us."

She placed her palm to his chest.

Her hand glowed faintly.

"Your fight was never in vain," she said. "It just wasn't the final stanza."

She paused.

"Your son won't be ready," she said softly. "He'll be chosen."

Zorion's eyes welled.

But there was no shame left.

Just awe.

—

Clouds drifted across the moon like forgotten prayers.

In the treeline, far beyond vision, silver eyes opened.

Blinking sideways.

Then disappearing.

The Damlyas had found scent.

But not the truth.

20

Where the Silence Trains You

"Silence is also speech." - West African Proverb

The rainforest didn't welcome. It tested.

Mist clung to Sakira's skin like breath from the earth itself. Her hoodie was soaked through, her steps slow but steady. Insects hummed in layered rhythm, like drums played by invisible hands.

She followed the trail deeper, past tangled roots and whispering leaves, until the path opened into a clearing. There, half-shadowed by a massive tree, stood a woman.

LeeLeigh.

Her body shimmered with sun-slicked heat, wrapped in tribal cloth woven into battlegear. A blade of light rested across her back. She looked no older than twenty-five, but her eyes held centuries.

"Nobody walks this deep," LeeLeigh said, "unless they're runnin' from somethin'... or called by the roots."

"I ain't runnin'," Sakira replied. "And roots don't call me. I come because it's time."

LeeLeigh's smile was half amusement, half recognition. "Time's a hoop. Keeps rollin' 'til you decide to step inside it."

She stepped forward, slow and deliberate. There was no threat in her movement — only ancestral weight.

"I was sent to find you," Sakira said. "Jazz sent me. The Damlyas are here. We need you."

LeeLeigh tilted her head. "You walk like you know something I don't. But your energy's riddled with hesitation. Your soul's knockin', but I ain't sure you answered the door yet."

"I'm here, ain't I?" Sakira said. "Three buses, one sketchy ferry, and a canoe I paddled solo through snake-infested swamps. That's not a girl running. That's a warrior rollin' the dice."

LeeLeigh leaned in until their foreheads nearly touched. She placed two fingers on Sakira's temple.

Energy flared. Then silence.

"There's fire in you," she whispered. "But it's scared of burning the wrong thing. We'll fix that."

—

The training grove was ringed with torches. Moonlight filtered through the canopy, casting long shadows across the dirt.

LeeLeigh slammed her staff into the ground. "Show me who you are when no one's watching."

"No breathwork? No jungle crystals? No sage playlist?" Sakira asked.

"This is the playlist," LeeLeigh said. "Welcome to the remix. Fight."

They clashed.

Sakira was fast, but reactive. LeeLeigh moved like memory — redirecting, flowing, striking with precision. Sakira stumbled on an emotional flinch. LeeLeigh swept her hard.

"You're leading from trauma memory," she said, standing over her. "But healing moves different. Can't win with wounds you won't name."

"You always talk like a poet and a warning label?" Sakira panted.

"Only when I meet someone worth the page."

They fought on. Five minutes of rhythm and revelation. At the end, they shook hands. Helped each other up. A warrior's smile passed between them.

—

Night fell.

They sat cross-legged by the fire, glowing stones flickering between them. Moths orbited the flame like tiny dancers.

"So why'd you vanish?" Sakira asked. "The Warriors needed you."

"Needed me?" LeeLeigh said. "Or needed to believe the light could show up without a permission slip?"

She paused.

"I wasn't hiding. I was listening. Silence's a teacher — if you stop trying to outtalk it."

Sakira nodded slowly, turning the words over like a mango seed.

"But then you showed up," LeeLeigh said. "And that's how I knew the frequency was shifting."

She reached into a carved wooden box and pulled out a pendant — star-metal strung in woven vines and glyph-thread.

"This don't crown you," she said. "It reminds you. Of the fire that sings louder than fear."

Sakira closed her fingers around it. When she looked up, her eyes were clear.

"Then next time fear knocks," she said, "I'll be the one that answers — with my bare feet, baritone, and no apology."

They rose together.

Behind them, the jungle hummed — not menacing, but awake.

Above, the moon hung like it was watching two stars remember themselves.

—

Abidjan pulsed with rhythm.

Jazz moved through the market like peace with purpose. Mangoes glistened. Djembe echoes bounced off painted walls. A vendor handed her a cloth printed with interlocking spirals. No words. Just recognition.

She nodded. Paid. Kept moving.

Down a vine-shadowed alley, she found the bamboo curtain. Two breaths. Then she stepped through.

—

In the courtyard beneath a mango tree, Khamari trained alone.

His staff sliced the air with grace honed in exile. He didn't just move — he remembered.

Jazz watched silently, arms crossed, chin low. Waiting for the right beat drop.

Khamari's next strike stopped a half-inch from her temple.

"I don't entertain ghosts when I'm breathing," he said.

"Then exhale deeper," Jazz replied. "I'm not a ghost. I'm the part of you that was waiting for you to stop hiding."

He studied her. Wiped his brow. Stepped back.

"I've seen messengers arrive when the war's already started," he said. "Bringing flags instead of fire. What makes you different?"

"I didn't come to pull you into battle," Jazz said. "I came to remind you what the silence trained you for."

He said nothing.

But his eyes thawed.

—

Inside the dojo, the wood floors were carved with glyphs. A shrine glowed in the corner — candles, red ash, folded robes, a broken mask.

Khamari wrapped his hands in cloth. Jazz knelt beside him, tracing the ash.

"You weren't hiding," she said. "You were anchoring the signal — until we tuned back in."

She paused.

"Now the rhythm's aligning. And the noise is about to catch up."

"I'm no leader," Khamari said. "Last time I followed instinct... people burned."

"Then let's lead by vibration, not direction," Jazz said. "We don't need a general. We need a frequency the Damlyas can't decode."

He nodded once.

"Then I need to fight you," he said. "To know who you are."

—

They sparred.

Breath syncing. Blades flashing like memory.

Jazz moved low, fluid. Khamari pushed. She redirected.

They danced across rooftop tiles, each step a test.

Final move: her staff stopped at his throat.

He didn't flinch.

He nodded.

—

They sat side-by-side on the steps as night fell.

"I used to believe I'd die quiet," Khamari said. "Somewhere no one would remember my rhythm."

"You still might," Jazz said, smiling. "But at least this time... the silence will know your name."

She laughed. Honest. Brief. Then stood.

Khamari exhaled.

"Then tell the light," he said.

He paused.

"Africa stands again."

21

Back Into Light

"Every bush is a man." – Bajan (Barbadian) Proverb

Newark breathed in shadows.

Ty moved through the backstreets with calm heat — head down, heart up. The streetlamp above him flickered like it couldn't make up its mind. Graffiti tags glowed faintly on the brick wall beside him, but one shimmered in rhythm: the light glyph, half-faded but alive.

He stopped near a shuttered laundromat.

From the dark, Sakira stepped out, sipping a tall mango Jarritos with the casual energy of someone who could dodge bullets or throw them.

"About time," she said. "I was two sips from leaving you on read in two dimensions."

Ty smirked. "Blame the guy arguing with a fire hydrant about climate change. I think he had a point."

A soft crunch landed beside them.

Jazz had dropped from above, silent as breath, her presence folding into the night like it belonged there.

"Good," she said. "The team's assembled. Now can we start talking like the planet's deadline ain't snoozing anymore?"

They chuckled. Then their eyes met. And shifted — on beat — into focus.

Ty opened his palm.

A soft-glow crystal rose, hovering. The air warped into a 3D topography of Earth, pulsing with faint golden signals.

"Khamari's in," Jazz said. "Says nothing. Thinks everything. Moves like thunder forgot how to announce itself."

"We needed him," Ty said. "Sounds like he could wipe out an army and still fold a shirt perfectly."

"One more find," Sakira added, "and we're Voltron. Or Wu-Tang. Or one big cosmic group text with bad reception."

They laughed. But Ty stayed quiet, watching the pulses swirl inward.

Toward him.

"What if I'm the one link too weak to hold the chain?" he said softly.

No melodrama. Just truth. It landed like gravity.

Jazz didn't flinch. "You keep calling it weight," she said. "But maybe it's your wings. Only feel heavy till you remember you can fly with them."

Ty studied her. Then Sakira. The glow hummed louder.

"I ain't afraid of losing," he said. "I'm afraid I win... and still feel like I lost me."

A pause.

Sakira's voice dropped low. "Then stop aiming for perfection. Just be light enough for the ones close enough to feel you."

A shriek cut through the silence — cat or saxophone, no one knew.

"Was that... Hardley Parker?" Ty asked.

"Nah," Sakira said. "That's Ms. Wiggins' demon kitten. Sound like Miles Davis had a bad breakup in her basement."

Laughter cracked the tension. The spell breaker they needed.

They formed a circle.

Palms out.

The crystal glowed warmer. The city seemed to pulse around them — slowly, surely.

"Three awake," Jazz said. "More out there dreaming loud."

"And when the Damlyas come..." Ty began.

"We ain't hiding," Sakira said. "We're harmonizing. With fists and thought and heart."

Ty nodded. "My parents used to tell me about a team of underground Warriors of Light. Said if I ever needed them, I could rely on them. That time has come."

He looked up.

"Our next stop is London."

They leaned in, hands together over the light.

The crystal flared.

A gust of energy rippled upward — like smoke learning to become a star.

On the wall behind them, three shadows stretched long.

One for Newark.

One for exile.

And one... almost trembling.

But we couldn't see why.

Not yet.

22

The Whisper That Breaks the Circle

"What sweet in goat mouth does sour in he behind." –
Trinidadian Proverb

Everlion pulsed with dread.

Above the Crimson Trenches, the sky churned like
rotted blood. Spikes of obsidian architecture rose into
lightning that never struck — it lingered, twitching like a
thought too dangerous to finish.

Inside the Black Citadel, the Memory Chamber
stirred.

A basin of liquid data rippled on its own. Footage
hovered above it — Ty's rooftop glow, a glyph painted in
London, a woman's face caught mid-thought. Then
Sakira's image formed. Not surveillance. A transmission.
Half hologram, half prayer.

Vorrak's voice drifted in, quiet and amused.

"Even fire can be loyal," he said. "All it takes is the
right match... and a forgotten burn."

In the Transmission Cocoon, Sakira knelt in her true
form — obsidian-stitched gold, eyes dimmed like she

hadn't slept in days. A Damlya crystal hovered before her, absorbing every word.

"He trusts me," she said. "Deeply. Almost recklessly. I gave him truth in the shape of comfort, and he drank it like water."

She paused.

"Another week, he'll lead them straight into the throat of prophecy. And never see the fang behind the blessing."

Her hand trembled. She hid it.

But the crystal saw.

Suddenly, Vorrak's voice cut in — not through speakers, but inside her mind.

"You speak your duty like a poem," he said. "But even poems betray their authors."

Sakira jolted. Her composure slipped.

"I've given you exactly what you asked for," she said.

"But not what you feel," Vorrak replied. "And now the others question your rhythm."

A pulse surged through her. Her eyes flashed. They were watching her too.

"You miss them," Vorrak said. "That rooftop silence when no one needed saving. Just presence."

He paused.

"Tell me... have you convinced yourself yet?"

Her fingers went to her chest — to the necklace LeeLeigh had given her.

"They made space for me," she whispered. "Even when I wasn't sure I existed."

"So did we," Vorrak said.

Then the war room unfolded.

Vorrak walked through a map made of sound. Four zones echoed: London. Newark. Colombia. Ivory Coast.

"They think they assemble family," he said. "Let them."

He raised his staff.

"We'll feed the illusion. Breathe false frequency into their spine. And when Ty stands tall enough to carry the title..."

He slammed the staff.

Everything went dark.

"...we'll remind him that prophets don't survive the spotlight."

Back in the cocoon, the crystal pulsed again.

A new command looped: *Proceed to London. Phase Two active.*

Sakira breathed heavy. The glyph necklace in her palm glowed, then dimmed. She almost crushed it.

But didn't.

"I was just trying to belong," she whispered.

Behind her, a Damlya monitor flickered.

It wasn't just Vorrak watching.

Someone else had started tracking her too.

The transmission cut.

Her consciousness snapped back to Earth.

From space, Earth rotated peacefully.

But Everlion's shadows now crawled across its surface in real time.

And in London... a beacon flashed unknowingly.

Like a lighthouse accidentally inviting a storm.

Portals and Passports

Midnight over the Atlantic.

Ty stared out the plane window. Stars scattered across the sky, but one flashed unnaturally — like it was tracking him.

Jazz reclined with a comic book about post-royal Jamaican sorcerers. Sakira sat stiffly, one eye twitching, trying to be unreadable.

"I still think we could've just teleported," Jazz said, not looking up. "Ty's glowing, like, weekly now."

"Maybe one day," Ty replied. "Can teleport prophecy, but not checked baggage."

Sakira chuckled. "Well hurry it up then."

Ty winced. Jazz raised an eyebrow.

"We should all get some sleep," she said. "Long journey ahead."

"Yes, Mum," Sakira muttered.

Beat.

Jazz turned to Ty. "You okay?"

"You ever feel ready and raw at the same time?" he said. "Like somebody handed you both a crown and a throat to protect?"

"Every time I read your aura," Jazz said. "It's like hugging a live wire wrapped in prayer beads."

Sakira's fingers traced her necklace.

She stiffened.

Ty noticed.

Didn't speak.

Minutes later, Izzy appeared via hologram — seated in a war room filled with glitching maps. London shimmered behind him.

"ETA London: 06:44," he said. "Watch the fog near Thames. It's coded lately. Pixel patterns. Somebody's manipulating atmosphere."

"Have a British breakfast ready, my G?" Jazz asked.

Izzy smirked. "Got you. It's gonna be invisible. New thing I'm trying out."

"Any allies on arrival?" Sakira asked.

"Once you get to the bookstore front," Izzy said. "Blake & Sons. Caribbean auntie runs it. If she side-eyes you, that's your clearance."

Suddenly, the cabin dimmed.

All speech faded into vibration.

Ty saw something outside the plane — four glowing Damlya figures hovering like constellations. They didn't attack.

They listened.

Ty's glyph flashed involuntarily.

Everyone felt it.

"They know we're coming," Jazz said.

"They've always known," Ty replied.

—

Morning. Heathrow Airport.

The trio walked through customs like shadows. Ty carried nothing. Sakira wore mirrored shades. Jazz hummed to herself.

A guard scanned their documents. His machine sparked briefly, then cleared.

"You folks in some kind of performance group?" he asked.

"Only on weekends," Jazz said. "Tuesday through prophecy, we freelance war."

The guard blinked.

Stamped their passports.

—

London.

A black cab rolled into the city.

Fog curled around the streets. Glyphs shimmered briefly on signs. A raven perched on a lamppost, watching.

Sakira looked out the window.

"It begins," she said quietly.

Ty leaned forward.

London breathed beneath him.

Heavy.

Brilliant.

Waiting.

23

Where the Concrete Hums

"Cat luck ain't dog luck." – Bajan Proverb

South London moved like a cipher.

Ty, Jazz, and Sakira threaded through the back alleys of Peckham, hoodies up, headphones on, every movement tuned. No one spoke unless it mattered. The city pulsed with coded sound — motorbike revs, aunties with gold teeth on Bluetooths, garage and bass slicing through fog from a corner store radio.

A CCTV camera sparked briefly overhead.

Hacked. Just for them.

Ty glanced up. "Whole city watching," he murmured. "Feels like it knows something I don't."

"It does," Sakira said. "It knows how to survive without an audience."

Ty looked at her. Straight face. No reply.

They kept walking.

—

The entrance to the resistance was hidden in plain sight.

Blake & Sons. A dusty bookstore with a Jamaican flag in the window. Vinyl racks near the back. An old woman nodded once, slid a copy of a Dick Gregory book backward on the shelf.

Click.

A trap door opened beneath the rug.

—

The London Stronghold was carved in concrete and memory.

Dim violet LEDs lit the bunker. Pirate radio gear buzzed in one corner. Spray tags read: *Light is Listening.* A holographic map of the globe glitched, then corrected itself when Ty stepped closer.

A woman emerged from the shadows — mid-thirties, Bantu knots, gold septum ring, drill jacket zipped to her clavicle. Izzy. She'd built this place on instinct and stolen data.

Ty walked in. Said nothing.

"WOLA," Izzy said. "Never thought the one with the pulse would be this quiet."

"Didn't realize prophecy came with expectations," Ty replied. "And a guest list."

Izzy smirked. "It doesn't. But rhythm? Rhythm always answers — whether or not you're ready."

She tossed him a data key.

The screen glowed brighter in his palm.

Only his palm.

—

Jazz laid out operative maps. Sakira sank into a quiet corner, fingers tapping, processing. Ty stood at a narrow opening in the wall, looking out over the Thames.

"If they touch this city," he said, "they'll find out what silence sounds like when it fights back."

Izzy didn't respond.

She didn't need to.

She saw it.

Ty wasn't waiting to become the leader.

He already was.

—

Intel dropped like whispers.

Sakira overheard a signal trace from Everlion. Paused mid-step. Almost seen.

A young rebel reported glowing figures in Croydon last week — "like the sky bent inward."

A child sketched a glyph Sakira recognized.

She folded the paper before anyone else saw.

—

Later, in a moment of breath and banter, Ty watched old CCTV footage of himself sparring in London.

"Man," he said. "My form was trash back then. I moved like grief in sweatpants."

Jazz grinned. "Now you move like someone who knows somebody's watching."

"Still better than Rico's punches," Sakira added. "Man fought like he was asking the air for permission."

They laughed.

Even Izzy cracked half a smile.

—

Night fell.

The group stood on the rooftop, looking out over London's glow.

"You know they're not just coming for you," Izzy said. "They're coming for belief itself."

Ty nodded. "Then I better show belief knows how to throw hands."

Sakira's smile tightened.

Her hand grazed the glyph necklace LeeLeigh had given her.

Not flinching.

But flickering.

—

Below ground, the resistance maps glowed brighter.

Ty's glyph now mirrored across at least five other cities.

But one signal pulsed slightly... wrong.

Near Sakira.

24

The Arrow That Hesitated

"Trouble don't set like rain." – Guyanese Proverb

Fog rolled like it had a place to go.

The van rumbled down a gravel path, moonlight painting the English countryside in grayscale. Ty watched the GPS pulse silently, but his focus was elsewhere.

"He's close," he murmured. "Feels like the trees know his name."

Jazz sat in the passenger seat, eyes closed, listening inward. Khamari watched out the rear window, unmoving. Sakira tapped rapidly on her tablet, but the screen showed something beneath the map — a faint Damlya code woven like a whisper.

Ty saw it.

Said nothing.

Yet.

—

Crows scattered as they approached the warehouse.

Broken windows. Rusted metal whispering old battles. The door creaked open.

SaJai stood in shadow, bow drawn, aimed without tremble. His eyes scanned all four. Didn't blink.

"You lost," he said, "or suicidal?"

"Neither," Jazz replied calmly. "Just tired of knocking on doors that forgot what shelter means."

SaJai lowered the bow. Barely.

His accent was clipped. Military. But his soul moved like a monk.

"Three of you vibrate clean," he said. "But her?"

He nodded at Sakira.

She smiled. Disarmed, but not disarming.

"My rhythm's complex," she said. "Not corrupted. You want purity, go ask a ghost."

Ty stepped forward, showing his Warrior of Light pendant.

"I knew who you were before you arrived," SaJai said.

"We didn't come to fight," Ty said. "We need as many Warriors as possible. The war's gonna land whether you're armed or not. The Damlyas are coming. You know what they've come to do."

"War never needed my permission," SaJai replied.

The wind stopped.

Like breath holding.

Then—

CRACK.

Distorted energy blades slashed through the air. A bolt of lightning folded sideways midair and shattered a tree.

The Damlyas had arrived.

—

The battle was tight. Cinematic. Brutal.

SaJai fired arrows with rhythmic precision. Each one glowed upon release, bending mid-flight like they remembered something.

Jazz moved like Tai Chi in rage, slicing through a Damlya with water-formed daggers.

Khamari absorbed a blow, then spun it back with an elbow strike that disintegrated his attacker mid-motion.

LeeLeigh fought like a whisper sharpened into steel — Jet Li inspired, deadly, graceful.

Sakira fought... hesitantly.

Her reactions lagged. Two seconds too slow.

Ty clocked it.

Then—

A blade nearly pierced Jazz's side.

Ty screamed.

And time paused.

Only for him.

The world became watercolor static. Sound dropped out. Even breath froze.

Ty turned.

Moved Jazz two steps back.

Redirected SaJai's next arrow mid-air.

Time resumed.

The arrow hit the Damlya square between the eyes.

Khamari stared at him. "What was that?"

"I don't know," Ty said. "But it felt like the world waited... until I told it not to."

—

The final blow came fast.

A massive Damlya began to self-destruct.

Sakira shut it down early — an energy spike none of them had seen before.

They stared at her.

Jazz narrowed her eyes. "Since when could you do that?"

Sakira deflected. "Since I realized I had to."

She walked off.

Ty watched her harder now.

Not with suspicion.

With preparation.

—

The fight left them bruised. Bloodied. But breathing.

They stood outside the warehouse, moonlight filtering through splintered beams.

SaJai loaded his last arrow back into the quiver. Stepped forward. Offered his hand.

"You need a strategist," he said. "I need a reason to believe again."

Ty took his hand. Nodded once.

"Let's make the war regret showing up."

—

They walked through mist.

Five rhythms.

One pulse.

But behind them, Sakira's shadow stuttered.

For a split second... it didn't follow.

Then it did.

But we saw it.

25

Where the Future Waited

"We do not rise to the level of our expectations; we fall to the level of our training." – Archilochus

The London Underground had forgotten its name.

Tile mosaics peeled like old skin from curved walls. LED rigs dangled from makeshift beams. The station had become something else — part hideout, part dojo, part sermon. The rhythm of light matched the sound of breath.

They trained.

They remembered.

They became.

—

SaJai scrawled tactical diagrams across an old subway map — ambush paths, sniper zones, frequency gateways. His fingers moved like he was drawing from memory, not theory.

Khamari taught Jazz how to strike without rage. Her movements flowed through patterns, not punches. She moved like someone learning to fight with forgiveness.

Sakira trained alone.

She punched shadows.

Her rhythm was sharp.

But her focus cracked.

A flicker in her aura.

No one else saw.

—

Ty stood at the edge of the platform. Eyes closed.

He hovered.

Briefly.

Shaky.

Then laughed — startled by his own lift.

Flashbacks folded in.

Eight-year-old Ty balancing on a bamboo pole. Novi's voice: *"It's not about what you lift. It's about what you stop dragging."*

Then Zorion, throwing sand in his eyes mid-lesson: *"You think an enemy waits for comfort?"*

Back in the present, Ty flickered.

Then vanished.

Three full seconds.

Invisible.

He reappeared, gasping, grinning.

The team stared.

"You're not becoming something new," Jazz said. "You're remembering."

—

Later, near the tracks, Ty and Khamari sat side by side, arms resting on knees.

"When I was captured," Khamari said, "they didn't break my body. They gave me silence. Let it echo until I started filling it with doubt."

Ty nodded. "What brought you back, WOLA?"

"A rhythm I forgot I had," Khamari said. "And a woman who reminded me that even broken drums echo."

—

In the corner near old ad maps, SaJai cleaned his bow in silence.

Sakira watched him. Arms folded. But softer tonight.

"Why do you flinch before you strike?" SaJai asked.

"Because part of me still hopes we're wrong," Sakira said. "That they're not... monsters."

"You're not wrong to think that," SaJai said gently. "You're just unfinished."

She looked down.

That one hit.

—

The map glowed.

Pulse points across Europe lit up — Damlya stations embedded in Earth's skin. One blinked brighter than the rest.

North Sea.

—

The safehouse pulsed with quiet urgency.

A cracked concrete table. Blueprints of neighborhoods. Conduits drawn in chalk. Scrolls half-unfurled. Vinyl static played under thunder from a busted speaker.

The squad gathered: Ty, Jazz, Sakira, Izzy, SaJai, LeeLeigh, Khamari.

Battle-scarred.

Breath-ready.

Ty stood. Glowing faintly.

"Look," he said. "We don't know when. We don't know where. But we know why they're coming."

"They want what the WOLAs carry," LeeLeigh said. "Soul. Rhythm."

"That fire that made jazz and graffiti and joy that's unstoppable," Sakira added.

"They tried to mute galaxies," Jazz said. "Earth ain't just next. It's the final verse."

"But they ain't ready for this remix," LeeLeigh said.

"So what," Khamari asked. "We wait?"

Ty shook his head. "We live. Every move we make with truth? That's resistance."

"Every beat we drop with soul?" Izzy said. "That's war."

"Every time we rise with each other?" Ty said. "That's prophecy."

SaJai closed his notebook. "So we build. Train. Dance. Love. 'Til they show up and realize—"

"They ain't taking nothing from a world that already claimed itself," LeeLeigh finished.

"We weren't chosen to be perfect," Ty said. "We were born to be ready."

SaJai reached for a stick of chalk.

On the crumbling wall behind him, he wrote:

LIGHT BENDS. LIGHT FIGHTS. LIGHT STAYS.

He turned to the crew.

Their faces lit by flickers of soul.

When you find your rhythm, Ty thought, *you stop asking when the war's coming. You start becoming the answer to it.*

—

They walked side by side into the dark.

Hoodies up.

Energy pulsing.

Not fugitives.

Not myths.

A movement rising.

No permission.

Just rhythm.

Steady and unstoppable.

26

Catching Up to Prophecy

"A tree stands strong not by its fruits, but by its roots." –
Filipino Proverb

Fog slipped between the tree trunks like a secret being passed.

Novi and Zorion stepped through the brush, clothes torn, eyes raw with exhaustion — but not defeat. Their feet were bare. On purpose. The earth needed to feel them. And they needed to remember what it meant to feel the earth.

Below, in the valley, lights flickered.

A small village wrapped in warmth.

—

The villagers gathered quietly.

No words were needed. Recognition was older than speech.

An elder woman stepped forward, her eyes deep with memory. She laid a hand on Zorion's chest.

"Your heart runs fast," she said. "But it ain't running away. Let it settle. We keep those who carry truth… even when it's heavy."

Zorion nodded.

Not in agreement.

In surrender.

—

The training grove was hidden — ringed by torches and ancient stone.

Novi moved through the Way of Rhythm, Soul-Fu, the alien martial art she had carried across galaxies. Her movements fused capoeira, kung fu, and motion drawn from star maps. Her feet disturbed the earth in spirals. Her breath matched the wind.

Zorion tried to follow.

His timing was rough.

He was too angry.

Too loud.

"It's not about defeating the enemy," Novi said, correcting him. "It's about reminding the body it doesn't belong to fear."

"Then why does fear keep getting closer?" Zorion asked.

She stopped.

Walked toward him slowly.

Took his shaking hand.

"Because prophecy doesn't reward peace," she said. "It tests it."

—

The community rose.

Zorion taught children how to move through rhythm, not reaction.

A child sketched glyphs from memory — ones Zorion hadn't even learned yet.

Villagers planted crops in spiral patterns, the way Novi taught them.

At night, they raised their hands to the stars.

Not in worship.

In knowing.

—

Novi sat cross-legged.

Zorion sharpened a staff carved from oak.

He paused.

"Why here?" he asked. "Why stay?"

"Because faith doesn't follow the loudest path," Novi said. "It follows the one that listens."

She looked at him.

"You think the prophecy ended with you," she said. "But it started because of you."

She handed him a small pendant etched in symbols.

He held it.

We recognize it.

It's the same one Ty now wears.

—

At the edge of the rainforest, the trees whispered again.

But not in wind.

A Damlya scout crouched in blackened vines. Its form barely visible, blending into bark. Its eyes flickered silver-blue.

Watching.

Listening.

Waiting.

—

The village slept.

But in the wind, we heard a distant beat.

Not music.

Not drums.

A heartbeat made of prophecy.

And something else.

Marching toward it.

27

The Symphony of the Unfinished

"The one who holds the drum decides the rhythm." – Igbo Proverb

Everlion did not rotate.

Its sky contracted — like breath held too long. Obsidian towers spiraled upward, jagged and deliberate, piercing the atmosphere like broken tuning forks.

At the center of the Broken Altar, Vorrak stepped barefoot across scorched stone.

His army knelt in spirals.

Thousands of Damlyas.

They did not breathe unless he did.

—

"Have you ever heard a song that ends on the wrong note?" Vorrak asked, his voice calm, curious.

"Not wrong in sound. Wrong in truth."

He paused.

"It makes the air itch. It makes silence look back at you like you lied to it."

He turned slowly, eyes sweeping across the kneeling formation.

"That's what Earth is," he said. "A melody abandoned before the chorus."

He smiled.

"And all of them — their Warriors, their poets, their bleeding hope merchants — they keep humming it... like they'll land the key if they just believe harder."

His voice echoed across the mesa.

It wasn't volume.

It was permission to listen.

—

"I don't want conquest," Vorrak said, softer now. "I want completion."

"To find the songs that won't resolve... and end them."

"Earth will not resolve. So I am going to end it."

"To quiet stars that blink with wasted potential. To silence prophecies that stutter halfway through a sentence."

He stepped to the edge of a massive obsidian basin.

Inside: an ocean of shadow.

Earth rotated within it.

Ty's face flickered.

Then Sakira's.

"Earth is not a battlefield," Vorrak said. "It is a note held too long."

"And I? I am its composer."

—

He unsheathed a weapon forged of light and memory.

Held it motionless above the map.

"They teach resistance through fists," he said. "We teach it through restraint."

"They leap. We listen."

"They call Sakira a friend. But what they've called her is not who she was before the name."

"Let them place their trust in light."

He paused.

"But light doesn't lead."

"It just arrives late... and hopes the darkness had bad aim."

—

He waved a single finger.

A low frequency rumbled.

Spherical energy unfurled above the altar.

Five Earth cities appeared — pulsing, already fraying at their edges.

No targets.

No missiles.

Just sound.

A pure D minor note played.

Low.

Final.

Disrespectfully human.

"Send nothing," Vorrak whispered.

"Just remind them what it feels like to live out of tune."

"And when they beg for crescendo... plead for resolution, for clarity, for salvation..."

He lowered his hand.

"Cut the music."

Past the army.

Past Vorrak.

Past the black hole moon above.

Somewhere on Earth, a violin string snapped by itself.

Somewhere in Ty's chest... a rhythm stumbled.

The symphony had begun.

28

The Sound of Betrayal

"A broken drum has no echo." – Ethiopian Proverb

The crew emerged from the subway's underbelly.

Steam hissed from a cracked vent. The sky hung lower than usual — almost like it was listening.

Ty led.

Jazz flanked right.

Khamari covered the rear.

SaJai whispered intel into his comm, crisp and clipped.

Sakira lingered a beat behind.

Watching them.

And herself.

Then the wind cut out.

A silver glyph lit the pavement ahead.

Time folded.

Vorrak appeared.

Not descending.

Arriving.

Like a truth unpaused.

—

"Earth sings in colors it was never meant to know," Vorrak said. "I am here to render it monochrome. A silence... permanent and pure."

His voice was calm.

Cruel.

"I've come to silence the song the stars never should've sung."

—

The Damlya warriors phased in behind him.

Their armor whispered.

Not clanged.

Khamari clashed first — pure form against invisible rhythm. He landed one blow. Then stumbled.

SaJai fired glowing arrows into the alley's throat. Two exploded midair.

Jazz moved like water fire — her blade a blur of memory.

Ty and Vorrak collided.

No fists.

Just silence and movement.

—

Then the circling slowed.

Vorrak held up a pulsing device — glyphs spinning like a clock in reverse.

"You guarded the door," he said to Ty. "But left the key in your pocket."

He turned.

Everyone followed his gaze.

Sakira.

Her eyes were wet.

But she didn't deny.

She stepped forward.

"It wasn't supposed to go this far," she said, voice shaking.

Ty's whisper broke. "But you walked with us."

"You laughed with us."

"I felt it all," Sakira said, cracking. "And I still... I still sent them your rhythm."

Jazz moved to strike her.

Ty held her back.

Not with force.

With fear.

—

Ty doubled over.

Rage.

Loss.

Grief.

All unfiltered.

But he didn't collapse.

The ground pulsed.

Air went quiet.

His skin flickered — not light, not invisibility.

Clarity.

He looked up.

Eyes golden.

Chest still.

No longer asking to lead.

Just being.

"I begged for peace," he said. "But maybe some songs don't start with harmony."

—

He unleashed a burst.

Vorrak phased backward.

Smirking.

Bleeding dark light.

"So he's arrived," Vorrak said.

"Finally. What I've come for."

He grinned.

"I love this part of the album."

Then he vanished.

So did his soldiers.

—

Sakira didn't flee.

She knelt.

Didn't cry.

Just waited.

—

The crew stood shattered.

Not as a team.

As broken chords.

Ty walked past her.

Touched her shoulder once.

"You don't owe us an apology," he said quietly. "You owe yourself a reckoning."

And the silence answered him.

Because betrayal isn't loud.

It's precise.

29

The Betrayer and the Beat

"A lie travels until truth puts on its shoes." – Russian Proverb

The warehouse smelled like rusted trust.

A single bulb flickered overhead, casting shadows that didn't move. Sakira stood near a burnt-out window, her silhouette more ghost than shadow. The rain outside tapped a rhythm against the glass — not dramatic, just persistent. Like truth trying to be heard.

Ty entered slowly.

No fire.

Just weight.

She turned. Tried to meet his eyes.

Regretted it.

"Ty…" she began. "You have no idea what's at stake. I never wanted to betray you, but Vorrak had my family."

A flash — Denzil and Yvonne, locked in a Damlya cell. Cold light. No sound. Her brother's eyes wide with fear. Her mother's lips moving in prayer.

"He's had them since before I even knew your name," Sakira said. "I thought I could delay the damage. Limit the lies. But there were always more asks. And eventually... fewer choices."

Ty didn't speak.

His chest rose.

His eyes unreadable.

Not fury.

Not mercy.

Just impact math.

"I lied," Sakira said quietly. "But I never faked the rhythm. Every laugh. Every rooftop. Every moment? Was me... trying to matter."

Ty finally spoke.

"Nah. That's not what you were doing."

"You were trying not to vanish."

He paused.

"There's a difference."

—

Sakira stepped forward.

Braver now.

Or more broken.

She held out the glyph necklace — LeeLeigh's. The pulse in it faint. She didn't ask for forgiveness.

She just stood in it.

"I can't forgive you," Ty said after a long silence.

"But I understand."

"Help us now… and we save your family too."

Sakira nodded.

Slow.

A breath like she'd never taken one for herself before.

"I'll tell you everything," she said. "Where they're keeping the others. What's encoded in the portal tech. Even what Vorrak fears — though he'd never admit he does."

Ty stepped back.

"Nah," he said. "Yous an eeeeddiat. And I'd be one too to turn around and trust."

"Just sekkle. And be glad we don't end you now."

—

They exited the warehouse together.

Not side by side.

But not strangers.

Ty didn't offer his hand again.

Sakira didn't expect it.

Outside, the rain continued.

Not loud.

Just quiet punctuation.

Like truth tapping a beat against the silence.

30

Surrender or Symphony

"The storm makes the oak grow deeper roots." – Swedish Proverb

London breathed in sirens and steam.

The Warriors moved through quiet alleys, boots slicing fog. Khamari scouted ahead. SaJai checked position flares. Jazz walked with narrowed eyes, her blade humming faintly. Izzy gripped his nunchucks.

Ty led.

Steady now.

This was the walk of someone who knew sacrifice was near.

They reached the rooftops.

The city stretched below — glowing, pulsing, unaware.

Then—

BOOM.

A flare erupted in the sky.

Then another.

Then... silence.

From smoke, Vorrak and his elite Damlya phased in.

Like broken metronomes.

Quiet first.

Then violence.

—

The battle was brutal.

Emotional.

Cosmic.

Khamari and LeeLeigh leapt from rooftop to rooftop, flanking with momentum — but one Damlya clipped Khamari in his knee mid-air. He landed hard, rolled, and rose again.

Jazz formed a protective ring around SaJai and Sakira, her blade absorbing frequency blasts. Her movements were fluid, fierce — like memory sharpened into steel.

Sakira fought with redemption, not rage. She cracked two foes with pulse discharges, but one nearly crushed her before SaJai saved her with a well-placed arrow.

Ty began to glow faintly.

Rhythm pulsed from his skin.

The ground split, tossing them into smaller clusters.

Vorrak watched from a firelit ledge.

Unrushed.

Unbothered.

—

Ty stood alone.

Bruised.

But ready.

Vorrak dropped down.

Walked up slow.

His voice was a blade wrapped in honey.

"You're brilliant in pieces, Ty," he said. "Every scar of yours sings louder than your spine does. But this is the song. You don't get to hum forever."

He waved a hand.

Behind him, images flickered across the smoke:

Jazz on the ground.

Khamari trapped in a glyph cage.

SaJai and LeeLeigh surrounded.

Sakira bleeding from the shoulder.

Izzy fighting — but losing.

"You want to be a hero?" Vorrak said. "Fine."

"Then choose: Give me yourself. Your rhythm. Your breath. Your frequency. Your soul. And I let them go."

"Or keep dancing... and let the next chorus be one no one lives long enough to hear."

—

Ty closed his eyes.

Novi's whisper — *"You don't owe the world your soul. Only your truth."*

Zorion teaching breath control in silence.

Sakira laughing on the rooftop.

Vorrak offering a bloody hand, palm up.

Ty clenched his fists.

Then released.

He stepped forward.

"I surrender," he said softly.

Everyone gasped.

Even the Damlya flickered in confusion.

Vorrak's grin widened.

"Wise," he said. "Finally."

Ty knelt.

Then looked up.

"But I didn't say to who."

He slammed his palms into the street.

Energy erupted.

A golden wave radiated outward, disrupting Damlya glyph cages. Healing pulses bounced from his chest.

Vorrak reeled.

Unbalanced.

Hurt some.

Surprised a lot.

—

The battlefield glowed.

Warriors rose.

Ty stood at the center of a symbol that wasn't drawn.

It grew from him.

His rhythm was no longer reactive.

It was command.

But Vorrak's eyes narrowed.

Not angry.

Amused.

The next move was coming.

And he knew this rhythm all along.

31

The Rhythm That Ended Fire

"When the music is over, the dance continues in the heart." – Balinese Proverb

The air hummed like it was nervous.

Buildings sagged like they'd seen too much. Lamplight bled green across cracked pavement. The city held its breath.

Ty stood in the center, smoke rising from his shoulders.

Behind him, the Warriors of Light gathered — wounded, unwavering.

Khamari limped forward, flicked a grenade casing away, electricity crackling in his palms.

Jazz locked blades, runes etched into her wrists glowing faintly.

Izzy adjusted her tech helmet, her eyes scanning for patterns.

SaJai checked his final arrow, fingers steady.

Sakira cracked her neck. Her ribcage bruised, but her grin sharp. She nodded at Ty.

From the haze, Vorrak emerged.

Elegant.

Eerie.

"You've danced well," he said. "But even rhythm gets tired."

—

Ty didn't answer.

Not yet.

Behind the silence, memory stirred.

Novi's whisper: *"You don't owe the world your soul. Only your truth."*

Zorion's calm: *"The wind don't brag, but it moves mountains. Be like that."*

Jazz's fire: *"Your name isn't weight. It's weapon. Stop apologizing for it."*

Vorrak smirked. "You fight like you matter. That's adorable."

Ty stepped forward.

"I'm not your myth," he said. "I'm the remix."

"I'm Ty from London, bwoy. Front rooms lit with incense and old school reggae dubplates. Grew up watching kung fu flicks with my dad and learning the Way of the Rhythm. Beats that taught me more than schools ever could."

"I wasn't chosen by prophecy."

"I chose me."

—

The earth answered.

Ty levitated.

Dust coiled.

Basslines pulsed from the pavement like ancient drums awakening.

Then—

Khamari slammed both fists down, sparking a shockwave that paralyzed a Damlya mid-lunge.

SaJai fired his final arrow straight through a glyph — it sang as it split the air, collapsing the trap around them.

Sakira vaulted from rubble, her blade dragging heat behind it — a swipe fueled by rhythm, not rage.

Izzy meditated. Three identical Izzy spirits emerged from her body, wisecracking as they fought.

Jazz and LeeLeigh leapt beside Ty, swords drawn, and auras syncing to his heartbeats.

They didn't just attack.

They harmonized.

"He's not just glowing," Sakira whispered.

"We all are," LeeLeigh replied.

Ty breathed steady.

"Every scar they gave me? I turned to tempo. Every lie they told? I remixed into truth."

"Now we're the beat they can't outrun."

He turned to the team.

"We're not soldiers. We're frequencies."

"Time to amplify."

The Warriors nodded.

A unified stance.

A wave erupted — not just from Ty, but from each of them, tuned into one chord, one purpose.

They breathed as one.

—

The battle began.

LeeLeigh and SaJai tag-teamed Damlya generals with aerial double kicks and synchronized elemental blasts.

Jazz channeled wind and fire, moving like tai chi caught in a hurricane.

Sakira reconfigured a fallen glyph into a vortex decoy, throwing it into Vorrak's elites.

Izzy sparred with hologram versions of herself, cracking jokes mid-combat.

Ty launched shockwaves through the ground — each footstep pulsing like a sonic boom.

Vorrak approached mid-fight, unfazed.

"You still want to write your own ending?" he said. "Then let me be your ink."

—

Ty and Vorrak clashed.

Aerial sequences defied gravity.

Vorrak weaponized memory — hurling echoes of Ty's past doubts as blade strikes.

Ty responded with silence.

Each dodge synced to meditation.

He vanished mid-strike.

Reappeared behind Vorrak.

Hands humming.

Not light.

Vibration.

"I don't fight you," Ty said calmly.

"I fight every time I doubted myself."

"You're just the loud version of my quietest fear."

—

Ty struck.

Not angrily.

Rhythmically.

Each motion had a purpose.

He redirected Vorrak's attack mid-air, shattering its intent.

A Damlya lunged — Ty hummed. Sound rippled. The creature froze mid-step.

Sakira was nearly hit — Ty disappeared, reappeared, moved her back like wind with his hands.

He levitated into storm clouds.

Electromagnetic spirals rippled from crown to heel.

His body didn't glow.

It chanted.

He spoke rhythm into the storm.

And the sky responded.

He formed a vortex of memory and breath, merging all five elemental energies from the Warriors.

"You wanted surrender?" Ty roared.

"Then take this — the part of me that refused to stop believing."

—

The world slowed.

Ty shut his eyes.

He remembered every loss.

Every note played out of tune.

Suddenly, a burst of color spiraled from his core.

Magnetic pulses collided.

He levitated.

His skin glowed.

Veins lit like auroras.

He became the embodiment of harmony — distorted and restored.

—

The fight crescendoed.

Ty dodged symphonic blade strikes that left sonic booms in their wake.

Vorrak slammed him through a skyscraper.

Ty rose.

They fought one-on-one — electromagnetic propulsion, kinetic poetry, dancing between death and redemption.

Vorrak overwhelmed him with chaotic pulse blasts.

Ty's ribs cracked.

His breathing stuttered.

"TY!!" a Warrior shouted.

Ty faltered.

Vorrak lifted him.

Threw him.

Ready to end it.

—

Ty, barely conscious, whispered:

"You wanted them out of tune..."

He pressed his palm to the earth.

A harmony rippled.

The Warriors of Light rose — synchronized in motion, voices, and fury.

Ty channeled it all.

Emotion.

Rhythm.

Memory.

His body became a vessel.

He crashed back into Vorrak with a maelstrom of chords and punches — rapid, metahuman speed.

A final blow.

A fitting death to a menace.

—

Caught in a rising vortex, Vorrak and the Damlyas twisted in dissonance.

Unable to maintain form.

Their beings began to burn.

Evaporate.

"Silence..." Vorrak gasped. "Isn't peace..."

Ty's final move was quiet.

An open-palm tremor that fractured the sky.

The monsters disintegrated into wisps of distorted notes.

The storm died.

The stars recalibrated.

32

The Last Whisper Before Tomorrow

"The dead are not gone; they are only invisible." – Akan Proverb

The vortex collapsed.

Vorrak was gone.

Darkness peeled away like wet fabric.

Rain fell — not violent, just cleansing. The kind that didn't ask for attention, only release.

Ty landed in the center of the cracked rooftop, breath steady. The ground beneath him was fractured, but his stance wasn't.

The Warriors gathered.

They exhaled together.

Like rhythm had been waiting for silence.

—

Sakira lay on a shattered section of rooftop.

Jazz knelt beside her, one hand on her shoulder, the other gripping her blade like it could hold time still.

Ty walked toward her.

No panic.

Just gravity.

—

Sakira's voice was weak, but clear.

"I fought with you," she said. "Not for redemption. But because the lies stopped working… and you didn't."

She coughed once. Blood. Then breath.

"You didn't let rhythm be rewritten. You danced it back into truth."

Ty knelt.

He touched her forehead.

Her skin was cold, but her eyes still held fire.

"Ty…" she whispered. "You are the WOLA. You are the hope we need."

"Stop the rest. Save the ones still dreaming."

She paused.

"And when peace comes…"

"Tell it I knew its name before it arrived."

Her eyes closed.

Her breath faded.

Like it left behind rhythm as a thank-you note.

Her glyph necklace pulsed once.

Then went still.

—

Ty stood.

No tears.

Just truth.

He lifted her necklace.

Wrapped it around his wrist.

"She didn't die trying to be perfect," he said softly.

"She died proving love was more dangerous than betrayal."

—

The Warriors formed a loose circle.

Khamari began to hum — low, steady, like a drum remembering its purpose.

Jazz tapped her blade against stone.

Three times.

SaJai raised his arrow to the sky and let it go — not to hit, but to float.

Izzy stood still.

Looked like strength in the flesh.

—

Ty turned to the group.

"This is not just victory," he said.

"This is a reminder."

"We're not Warriors because we win."

"We're Warriors because we walk forward — even when the people who helped us get here don't."

"This isn't peace yet."

"But it's a step toward it."

—

They walked through the wreckage.

No fanfare.

No speeches.

Ty led.

No crown.

No command.

Just presence.

—

London's sky cleared.

The next storm waited in shadow.

But this rhythm survived.

33

Rhythm Is a Weapon Too

"Hard ears pickney nyam rockstone." – Jamaican Proverb

Stadium lights flooded the playground.

Graffiti glowed like testimony. School gates stood wide open — like history ready to be corrected.

The courtyard pulsed.

Hundreds of students formed a live cipher circle. Hoods up. Phones out. Spirits loud. Some sat on bleachers. Others hung off stair rails. Heads nodded. Dreadlocks flopped. The beat was alive.

Ty stepped forward.

Hood down.

Face calm but charged.

He locked hands with Jamal, then Dante.

The energy was palpable.

"You missed three birthdays and one mixtape drop," Jamal said. "This crew been bleeding without you, my bro."

Dante smirked. "We heard you out there saving galaxies. Now come show these kids why the playground made you lethal first."

Ty nodded.

"Told you I'd be ready when it was time."

"Tonight... we rhyme to create memories. I'm assuming the victory."

"Not fame. Not flame."

"Just rhythm."

—

Across the lot, Rico's crew pulled up.

Varsity jackets. Heavy bass thumping from their speaker stack. Rico, older now, eyes cold. He saw Ty. Stepped into the cipher circle.

The crowd buzzed.

Classic '90s hip hop filled the air.

Backboards rattled under the boom of speakers.

Banners waved overhead: *Respect the Mic / Honor the Word*.

Jamal and Dante entered next.

Dap from every corner.

Ty stood calm.

Grounded.

Not like the return of a hero.

But the rise of a memory that never left.

"We waited," Jamal said. "Even when we thought you weren't coming back."

"I never really left," Ty replied.

—

At center court, a mic glowed like a truth detector.

Rico and his crew stood opposite.

No words exchanged.

Just nods.

Flexes.

Stares.

A local emcee stepped up to host.

"We've come to the final round and climax of the night," he said. "MC Ty vs. Rico the Roadman!"

"This ain't just about bars tonight."

"This is Newark's pulse auditioning for tomorrow."

"Respect. Power. Legacy."

"Let the rhythm decide."

The crowd roared.

Ty stepped into the circle.

Rico matched.

"Call it," the host said, flipping a coin.

"Heads," Rico said.

"Heads it is."

"First blow might be the last," Rico said. "So I'm rocking first."

"OOOOHHH!" the crowd shouted.

"DJ, drop that beat!"

—

The beat hit.

Boom-bap gold.

Bass breathing confidence.

Rico stepped up.

His verse cut sharp.

"Ty I'll steal your shine, believe that I'm dimmin' him

It's the big dog on campus, he's not even a citizen

Use you like a doormat, take your passport back

Hit Homeland Security and tell them... Deport That

Shortest to the tallest, I'm burying

Tell this guy the real football is Ameri

can

You ain't at home. Me? I'm invincible

How you think this clone gon' beat the original?

Cedar and Sedgwick, I was there when the kid ten

I think when, You was with your mates touring Big
Ben

It got more serious than a heart attack

When you realized you was in the home of where it
started at

You gonna fumble in the jungle with the hardest cat

I'm better made — get a blade, you wanna part of
that ?

I'm calm. 'Cause over there I see no bars

And not even the Feds could even get Rico charged!"

The crowd exploded.

Some cried.

Some filmed.

"OK OK OK!" the host shouted. "Yo, Ty — stage is yours, bruv!"

—

Ty stepped forward.

His voice was calm.

But his verse was a blade.

"Here's something to know — Rico not touching the flow, He's a liar — a Damlya — no substance or soul

You call me England, but I was never corny

I'm just the dog who came stepping on your territory

I'll bruise your ego when what you follow is pride

That pride I'll make you swallow .. but you still hollow inside

Listen. I move like Superman in Metropolis , flied and I write death, so here's where this novelist died

Ty's fresh!!! It's obvious, dropping kids — you shot and it's wide!

You'll read my rhymes like the Bible, when Solomon died!

I'm spreading light with the Warriors

'Cause a real king makes leaders, not followers

I flow iller — but everybody knows I'm the gorilla with brass knuckles giving him a thousand body blows

They tried to front on that — that's why I'm coming back like old pain

Break your armor, melt it, and wear it as a gold chain

I use my whole brain and mentally throw flame

How I took your spot... when I came here with no name.

And if hip hop started gritty and you learned the hard way

I'm cackling — 'cause now I'm battling Rico Suave!"

—

The crowd went wild.

Some cried.

Some filmed.

Ty bodied Rico so bad, he couldn't reach for another verse.

The crowd ran Rico out the gym.

He didn't fight it.

He nodded.

Not defeated.

Converted.

—

SaJai, LeeLeigh, Khamari, Izzy, and Jazz watched from the rooftop.

Stunned.

Moved.

The host grabbed the mic.

Lifted Ty's fist.

The crowd erupted.

—

Rico extended his hand.

Ty shook it.

Not as rival.

As rhythm rejoined.

The crews dapped up.

The cipher continued.

Above them, Ty's high school mural glowed faintly.

A new glyph painted beneath.

"Our voice isn't borrowed. It's ancestral."

The wall behind center court flickered.

Someone had painted a new message beneath the scoreboard:

"Bars can build bridges when fists fall short."

—

Silence at first.

Like reverence catching its breath.

Then hands rose.

Then fists.

Then cheers.

Rico stepped forward.

Placed his old mic down at center court.

Walked away.

—

Jamal spun one last record.

Dante shouted:

"From outer space to inner city — Ty brought it home!"

Kids chanted.

Teachers cheered.

Mics weren't dropped tonight.

They were handed forward.

Ty stepped outside into the night.

Rain began.

Not storm.

Just cleanse.

He looked up at the old school mural.

Someone had added a new line beneath it:

"Let the future rhyme with courage."

Ty smiled.

Not for the win.

But for the echo.

One built in rhythm.

One built to last.

34

The Last Verse Before The Storm

"The night hides a world, but reveals a universe." –
Persian Proverb

The crowd had settled.

The music was fading.

Ty slipped out the back doors of the gym, alone now, wrapped in reflection.

The night was quiet — not empty, just listening.

He walked slowly.

Past a lamppost tagged *Cipher Is Sacred*.

Past an old payphone booth, now a mural of Sakira — her eyes painted wide, her smile mid-verse.

He stopped.

Exhaled.

"We did it, Saki," he whispered.

—

The stars above didn't twinkle.

They moved.

Not randomly.

Rhythmically.

They pulsed in the same beat he'd rapped to — a pattern, a signature.

Someone... or something... had heard him.

One star went dark.

Then flickered red.

A sound rumbled from the sky.

Low.

Guttural.

Not thunder.

Not language.

A response.

—

Behind Ty, a soft voice broke the silence.

"You just woke up the next war... with a verse they thought would stay buried."

Ty turned.

A cloaked figure stood in the alley.

No footsteps.

No warning.

His hand glowed faintly.

On his sleeve: Sakira's family crest.

—

Ty didn't speak.

Didn't move.

The figure didn't advance.

Just stood.

Like punctuation at the end of a sentence no one was ready to read.

—

Inside the gym, Lola stepped onto the stage.

The lights dimmed.

The mic warmed beneath her hand.

She drew a breath—

and the world held its own.

THE END

ABOUT THE AUTHOR

Cymarshall Law was born in the United Kingdom to Jamaican parents, carrying the rhythm of two islands and one empire in his blood. In the early 1990s, his family moved to New Jersey, where the transition was anything but smooth — yet it was in that friction that his voice sharpened, his imagination expanded, and his purpose began to take shape.

He grew into one of New Jersey's most respected hip-hop artists, a prolific writer and performer whose catalog spans more than thirty projects and multiple vinyl releases with producers across the globe. His words have taken him around the world, touring stages from Europe to Asia to the Americas, earning him recognition as a true NJ Hip Hop icon and a staple of the culture.

Long before he ever wrote a book, Cy was a storyteller — in rhyme, in rhythm, in the cinematic worlds he built inside his verses. A lifelong lover of comics, sci-fi, and mythology, he saw himself as a writer who could inspire through imagination as much as through truth. His work blends the cosmic with the personal, the ancestral with the futuristic, always rooted in the belief that stories can shift culture and spark transformation.

Legacy of the Light is his third book, a continuation of the creative path he's walked since childhood: using words to illuminate, empower, and remind readers that the universe inside them is just as vast as the one above.